W9-CPW-209

SOMETHING WEIRD IS GOING ON

5/96 $6.95

FIC   Harris, Christie
HAR   Something Weird is
        Going On

DAVID CAMERON ELEMENTARY
615 ...
Victoria, ...
V9B 5Y1

Discard

SOMETHING WEIRD IS GOING ON

CHRISTIE HARRIS

ORCA BOOK PUBLISHERS

Copyright 1994 Christie Harris

All rights reserved. No part of this book may be reproduced in any form by any means without the written permission of the publisher, except by a reviewer who may quote brief passages in review.

Canadian Cataloguing in Publication Data
Harris, Christie.
Something weird is going on

ISBN 1-55143-022-3
1. Title.
PS8515.A789S65 1994   jC813'.54   C94-910706-9   PZ7.H23So
1994

Publication assistance provided by The Canada Council

Cover design by Christine Toller
Cover painting by Carl Coger

Printed and bound in Canada

Orca Book Publishers   Orca Book Publishers
PO Box 5626, Station B   PO Box 468
Victoria, BC Canada   Custer, WA USA
V8R 6S4   98240-0468

10 9 8 7 6 5 4 3 2 1

To T.A.H.
who helped me,
this one last time,
to handle a wild sea

ONE

Summer of 1983
Stanley Park, Vancouver, B.C.

Fresh as the nearby mountain meadows, her world was full of bird song. That stopped abruptly.

Xandra caught her breath. It was happening again: that sudden empty feeling, then that overpowering sense of a presence. Someone was watching her.

Warily she glanced around. And there was no one. Yet the park seemed newly hushed, its morning shadows deeper under the wide cedars. So, with one knee on the grass, Xandra kept very still, watching the alerted squirrels — as dark as her own dark hair, as dark as the lashes shadowing her intensely blue eyes. She scarcely moved her head, even when the feeling strengthened — that sudden, weird feeling that someone was watching her, here in the hush of the fragrant cedars. She knew, of course, that Gran was glancing at her now and then, and she knew why. Strangers — Gran called them "undesirables" — could be lurking among the big dark trees. But it was not Gran's eyes that were slowing her breath.

It wasn't *anybody's*. It was just her imagination, her totally overworked imagination. So after frowning at three arriving crows, Xandra turned her attention back to the squirrels, who were moving again like a stopped film back in action. The nearest squirrel was only a finger's length from her quiet hand, tiny forepaws lifted and bushy black tail curling above him. Suddenly he darted close enough to snatch a peanut and scamper off with it.

Xandra kept very still.

Another squirrel ventured closer and closer. Ran up her jeans. Snatched a peanut. Then leapt away.

She loved the squirrels. Scampering lightly up the trees, or bounding fluidly across the grass chasing one another, or venturing warily toward a proffered peanut, they were fun to watch. And who else was there to have fun with while Hughie was in daycare? She sighed a long, quiet, lonely sigh. Coming to a new place in the summertime was awful.

She caught her breath again. Someone *was* watching her. She could feel it, like a ghostly curtain wrapping its chill around her. The crows had gone still and as silent as the silent cedars. Even the squirrels had been struck motionless again, as if something alien had invaded their forest.

Quickly swivelling her head, Xandra glanced all around. And there was no one — no one but Gran, sitting over there on a bench in her loose purple dress, writing something in her notebook. Xandra frowned. Gran's crazy ideas were more than a little disturbing — especially to Mom. "Looking for something that isn't there," she had exploded. "Flying saucers. Spirit beings. Psychic phenomenon. Sessions with a hypnotist to find out what she was in a past life. Past lives!"

Remembering that outburst, Xandra swallowed. There couldn't have been past lives . . . could there? If people had past lives, what would they do between their lives? Float around as spirits or something, watching people who were still alive? Between their lives, could they be ghosts, watching people? Watching her now? She shivered, then resolutely shook off the shiver. It was just a cloud up there covering the sun, which was making it darker and chillier here at the edge of the trees.

Why did she always start scaring herself? Turning any situation into a drama starring Alexandra Warwick? Mom was right. It was silly.

Xandra put her attention firmly back on the squirrels. They were moving again, flowing over the grass. But in a wary way now? No. She frowned at her own silliness. Squirrels were always timid like that, always hesitant, always in character. It was just her imagination, thinking that someone was out there.

It was like when she was little, and lonely, and in a new place like now — so little and lonely that she had dreamed up a playmate, Flora Lee.

Flora Lee was just a misty memory now, just an imaginary girl a lonely child had conjured up to play with. But she had seemed to be real, there, at the bottom of the garden behind the Ontario house they had moved to when Xandra was four. The house they had lived in until this move to Vancouver.

The first time she had "appeared," Flora Lee had been as fierce as an outraged eagle defending its nest. Xandra, exploring her new home, had found a small plastic box on a rocky shelf almost hidden by the stones and flowers of the garden by the creek. And in the box she had found the pendant with its broken chain. The moment she touched it she had sensed its magic. And she had sat there for a long time, holding the pendant, wondering who could have hidden it . . . wondering if that someone would notice if Xandra took it away for awhile to show it to her dad.

Suddenly a voice had startled her, a faraway sort of voice. "That's mine!" the voice had said, so unexpectedly that Xandra had almost dropped the pendant. And when she glanced back over her shoulder, there was a red-haired girl deep in the shadows — as if she had materialized out of the vapour, like the genie in *The Arabian Nights*. "See. It says FLORA on it," the girl had said, her words a shadowy accusation.

But there wasn't a word on the pendant. There was nothing on its oval flatness except painted-on flowers: wild roses, forget-me-nots, violets and bluebells, all swirling mistily together with green vines under a glassy glaze. "It's . . . just . . . flowers," Xandra had dared to point out, bold as a squirrel confronting an outraged eagle. "It's . . . just . . . flowers."

"Flowers say FLORA. So . . . PUT IT BACK WHERE YOU FOUND IT." The voice rose to a screech.

Xandra had put the magical pendant back where she had found it, pretending to cry. What an actor she had been, even at four. After all these years, she could remember those sniffs, as she could remember the rest of the scene:

Flora Lee, mollified, had said, "You can take one pink." She was allowing Xandra to pick one of the aromatic flowers growing there, just as if it had been *her* house and not Xandra's.

"Okay," Xandra had answered, meek as a mouse — a character she was again playing. Maybe because once again she desperately wanted a friend.

Anyway, Flora Lee had become a weird friend for the next few years, always appearing deep in the shadows. And always the two had played until — suddenly — Flora Lee would not be there. Like the genie vanishing back into the urn, Flora Lee would be gone. But that was just the way she was. For years Xandra had truly believed in a real Flora Lee.

"Who are you talking to, dear?" Mom would ask when she had come silently over the grass.

"Oh . . . just . . . Flora Lee," Xandra would admit, reluctantly, because Mom did not like having that playmate around. She would narrow her eyes in disapproval.

Well, Xandra remembered, Flora Lee hadn't liked having Mom around either. She had not liked parents. Period. "They leave you!" she would rage whenever

Xandra dared to bring up the subject.

"They don't," Xandra would merely whisper her protest because Flora Lee was bigger and older and bossy and . . . and maybe she knew more about parents? "They . . . don't."

"They do so!" Always that strangely unnerving fury.

And Flora Lee had been right, hadn't she? Finally, just a year ago, Dad had left his family after a bitter fight with her mother. Dad. Who had always been his daughter's best friend. He had not minded having Flora Lee around, she remembered. Being an actor, he'd had no trouble with his daughter's make-believe. Once, as a small child, she had overheard her mom sounding pretty mad about the lack of playmates for Alexandra, who was spending "far too much time in make-believe."

Dad had just laughed it off. "Children often have an invisible playmate," he had assured Mom.

Invisible? Even as a small child, she had known what that word meant from her fairy tales. And she remembered being really cross with her father. "Flora Lee is not *imbisivle!*" she had told him.

But of course she was. Flora Lee had been just the most real of the characters Xandra had dreamed up in a lifetime of private dramas — dramas Mom had not appreciated when she had chanced on her child "talking to herself again."

"I wish you wouldn't carry on with this everlasting acting," Mom had been blinking back tears when she had said that — the terrible day when for that one and only time, she had called Dad a loser. "Acting!" she had stormed to her shocked daughter. "Look at your father, a loser. Damn it, Alexandra, he can't even support himself, much less his family . . . Oh! I didn't mean that," she had cried out before she'd rushed into her room and slammed the door shut.

Xandra had blinked back her own tears. Dad, her wonderful Dad, was a . . . loser? Actors were losers? Unless they got into the movies, of course, or into TV commercials and made lots of money, so they could support their family.

Mom would probably have liked to call Gran a loser, too, she thought now, glancing over at the park bench. Gran didn't spend all that much time in reality. But she turned out those books for kids, and the kids really liked them . . . "not enough to bring in much money, of course," Mom had once commented. "Your grandmother gets away with being a bit . . . different," she had pointed out that day, "because she has a good steady man to keep a roof over her head and food on the table."

Grandad, a retired school principal, was clearly one of the main reasons Mom had moved her children to Vancouver after the split with his son. Her children needed to have a good, sensible, solvent, down-to-earth male figure in their lives. And Grandad had time to take them for walks and visits to the aquarium; he enjoyed working with Xandra on her tennis at the free courts in Stanley Park. And he, too, didn't like Gran's "messing around with the unknown." Maybe he thought Dad — his own son — was a loser?

Loser. Xandra wished her mother had not used that word, even that one terrible time — a word that gave you nightmares about turning into a bag lady, like that tall, skinny woman who always wore a big winter coat and roamed the West End streets. Turning into that was a fate to make Xandra grab the scrub brush or the vacuum cleaner and be super-practical until the scary feeling wore off.

Dad was not a loser. He was the nicest person she knew. And his mother was great, too, even if she did wear purple pantyhose and get hypnotized to find out about her past lives. Xandra brushed off a tear. Dad's dreams were like her own; and she was going to go on hugging those dreams to her like the "blankie" she had long since discarded.

One of the squirrels caught her attention. He was scampering up a tall tree in rippling spurts, stopping to glance down at her. Probably wondering why she was sitting there like a stump.

Anyway, once she had made other friends back home, she had forgotten Flora Lee. She had forgotten even the pendant until the morning she and Mom and Hughie were leaving Ontario to move here. That morning, taking one last look around, she had gone down to the creek, bent down to smell the pinks and suddenly remembered the pendant she had so dramatically returned to its hiding place all those years before. With a sudden, daring feeling, she had pried the box out of the hidden rock shelf.

Running her fingers over the oval flatness of the pendant, she had sensed the old magic; she had delighted once more in the painted-on flowers: the wild roses, forget-me-nots, violets and bluebells. The pendant was really just plastic, but it was enchanted. And with an unaccountable sense that she was intruding, Xandra had slipped it into her pocket. She had actually caught her breath at daring to take Flora Lee's pendant as a keepsake for herself. And she had been carrying it around ever since while she watched for the right kind of chain to wear it with.

Now Xandra slipped her hand into her hip pocket. And there it was, smooth as polished marble. She stopped and looked around. Someone was watching her. She could feel it like a ghostly curtain wafting its chill toward her.

No! That was crazy.

She was just lonely again. As lonely as she had been that day when she was four. So her imagination had gone back into action, scaring up a drama. There wasn't anyone — or anything — watching her. "Let's go for a walk, Gran," she called out as she slipped her hand out of her pocket and abandoned the squirrels. "Could we maybe have something at the pavilion?"

"We certainly could." Gran dropped her notebook into her Mexican straw bag. "I was just thinking about a cappuccino."

"Hey. I'm psychic. And I'm desperate for a muffin." Of course. That's what was wrong with her this morning. In her hurry to get out of that empty apartment, she had skipped breakfast. And she should have known that was what it was when she'd had that sudden empty feeling. No breakfast.

Just the same, Xandra glanced back over her shoulder as she walked away. But she refused to believe that she felt a sort of tingling in her hip, right under the spot where the pendant lay waiting for its new chain.

"Great day for walking, Fiona O'Hare," she chirped

to Gran, who kept that maiden name for the by-line on her books, ". . . so your grandfather won't be embarrassed by them," she always quipped when he was around. Their family name, like her own, was Warwick.

"WARick," as Grandad pronounced it his brisk English way. "Your grandmother can call herself Fiona Finnigan Leprechaun O'Halleran O'Hare if she wishes," he always countered, "as long as it sells books."

Grandad was great. Since he was retired, he was always ready to take you walking or swimming or fishing or even travelling on the ferries. And if Gran cautioned him about not letting Hughie climb up on the ship's rail, he just patted her arm and said, "You sail your boat and I'll sail mine." You do your thing and I'll do mine.

Xandra sighed. How she wished Mom would say that to Dad.

Or to his daughter.

Glancing about at the magnificent trees and some smaller bushes, Xandra remembered that time with her father, two months ago, when he had taken his children to a friend's cabin for a weekend.

That Sunday morning, she and her dad had been standing by the lake near the trees, listening to the bird song, when he began to hum a melody, a lovely, swaying waltz melody. Then he added some words:

"DON'T touch my BERRIES and DON'T touch my TREES."

When he stopped suddenly, Xandra had urged him to sing more. "Dad, it's a beautiful song. Keep singing."

But he had shaken his head. And smiled. "Someday. Soon," he had promised.

That had stayed with her. Why hadn't he gone on?

TWO

"Gran, let's talk about Dad," she said as they started walking through the rose garden that sloped up toward the pavilion. This was the first summer he had not been with his family, and Xandra missed him terribly. "Tell me about when he was a boy. You know . . . the way he was."

"The way he was . . ." Gran's echo was wistful. "Well, as a boy, he couldn't see a sand dune without staggering across it, clutching his throat and begging, 'Water! Water!' He couldn't climb a tree without flinging himself through the branches like Tarzan. And when the woman next door left little Freddie with us, Connal . . . your father . . . always started right in on the stories, *being* the Wicked Witch or the Cowardly Lion. Mrs. Evans would pay him a nickel or two, though she'd already given him what he craved — an audience."

"He always wanted to be an actor, huh?"

"Yes, instead of a pilot or a deep-sea diver like the other boys."

Xandra silenced a sigh. Maybe if he had been a pilot or a deep-sea diver, maybe there wouldn't have been all those fights about money; maybe there wouldn't have been this split. Maybe if he had been different . . . No! She loved Dad just the way he was. And it was great to be a good actor, even if you didn't make it to Stratford or Hollywood. As she blinked back some tears, she felt her grandmother's hand squeezing hers.

"What we need is that cappuccino and that muffin," Gran said briskly as she led the way to the pavilion's verandah terrace, where hanging baskets were dripping with purple and rose fuchsias. "You find a table, dear, while I get the tray."

Wind chimes.

The crystal tinkle came, and was gone — like a wind stirring a tree, then leaving it as still and silent as a stage prop. Xandra's lips parted as the slightest of shivers went through her. But what was it with wind chimes? Why did they — sort of — make her shiver?

She stood still, looking at the hanging glass rods by the entrance. A plain, ordinary breeze had stirred them. Surreptitiously she licked a finger and held it up.

But there was no breeze. There wasn't a leaf stirring in the hanging baskets either. Another shiver went through her, making her as jumpy as a scared rabbit.

But there was a breeze later, along with threateningly dark clouds, as they walked home on the path by Lost Lagoon.

"It's going to rain," Gran said, urging Xandra along as she lingered at the spot where the beaver — a beaver who should not have been in the Lagoon — had cut down yet another of the beautiful weeping willows edging the water. "I hope it clears before it's time to pick up Hughie." She and Grandad had promised to take him to see the renegade beaver. Hughie was always shrill about that four-footed vandal.

The rain started after Gran had gone her way and Xandra was nearing Pacific Tower, the highrise where Mom had rented a friend's condo for six months while the friend was in Europe and Mom was starting her climb up the corporate ladder at Fenner Consolidated Wood Products, the head office of Mom's old firm. The six months would give her time to find a place where children weren't classified with cockroaches. It was probably only because Mom looked so sensible with her short hair and her classy suits that the management here was taking a chance on children in their fancy building.

The pelting rain sent Xandra scurrying toward the highrise. Maybe she would join the others at Lost Lagoon, but until then she would be alone in the suite, alone and wishing there was someone to phone, someone to groan about the rain with. But who was there? Until she started school, Xandra just did not know anybody in this strange city.

Alone in the suite, she practiced writing her name. Xandra? Zandra? Some of her friends thought it would be cool to have your name start with a Z. But there was no Z in Alexandra — her real name — was there? And besides, when she became a great actor, the big X was going to look sexy on the posters in the lobby — X-rated or something? So she was sticking with Xandra.

That settled, what could she do now? Alone in a tower like Rapunzel in the fairy tale. Her shoulders sagged in a theatrical sigh.

Then they straightened. She hauled out the old felt hat and the moustache Dad had given her in May when it had been his turn to have the kids and he had taken them to the cabin. The hat and moustache had been props for a dance routine she and Dad had been working on. Now, sighing at the memory, she put them on, thrust out her knees and started stomping around, hoping the THUMPS were sufficiently muffled by the thick rug.

"Put everything you've got into it!" Dad had urged, back there at the cabin, where you could raise the roof if you wanted to.

So now, putting everything she dared into it, Xandra belted out the song "There was a desperado from the Wild and Woolly West."

And when she got to the chorus and the desperado's "war whoop," her whoop might have startled the neighbours . . . if there had been any neighbours. Here, every adult raced out every morning with a brief-case like Mom's. And there sure weren't any other kids, or dogs. She yanked the hat down and really got into the spirit of the song, "WAHOO! WAHOOOOO!"

But, remembering what fun it had been back there in the cabin, the song just made her feel sad. With Dad gone, the routine was about as entertaining as footsteps in a dark, echoing, empty warehouse.

Xandra hid the props where Mom wasn't likely to run into them and turned on the TV. The place wasn't so gruesomely quiet with the TV on, so she kept it on until the sun finally came out. Then she fled the apartment to find Hughie and her grandparents at Lost Lagoon.

After walking slowly to the park entrance, Xandra sauntered along the lagoon path, watching the ducks and the geese and the stately swans. She could smell the wild roses before she got to the bush near a swan's nest in the rushes. Wild roses were so much more fragrant than the gorgeous blooms in the rose garden. Alert for bees, she sniffed one after another, while a red-winged blackbird kept an eye on her from a nearby weeping willow.

Once she had rounded the rosebush, Xandra could see her grandparents and she could hear Hughie. You could always hear Hughie. When he got excited, you could use him for the siren on a fire truck. Now, squatting at the edge of the water as he peered into it for some sign of the beaver, he could have scared that four-footed delinquent into joining the geese at the far side of the lagoon. He was LOUD.

When Gran waved to her, Xandra put a cautioning finger to her lips and ran silently along the path to surprise her brother. Coming up behind him, she said gently, "Boo!" A very gentle *boo*.

But he fell in. Actually, he pitched ahead into the water as if she had walloped him with a knapsack.

"Oh!" she burst out, "I'm sorry, Hughie." She hadn't touched the kid, but her *boo* must have really scared him. So she waded into the water and heaved him out, dripping water like a dunked dog.

"You pushed me!" he yelled.

"Hughie, I didn't."

The wet boy glared at his sister. "You did. You pushed me!" he insisted in a voice so loud that it lifted a pair of ducks off the water.

"Hughie," Gran said in a placating voice as she dabbed at him with her purple cotton stole. "Xandra didn't mean to push you."

He narrowed his eyes, looked accusingly at each in turn. "She did so."

"It was my fault," Xandra admitted. "But Gran, he slipped on the mud. I didn't touch him." That mud was probably one of the reasons the workers were starting to firm up the edges with rocks and concrete.

"I was pushed!"

Two policemen from the mounted patrol reined in their horses to glance down from the park road.

But it was Xandra who caught her breath. *I was pushed.* Somehow, those words — like the wind chimes

— were a haunting echo from . . . from where? From what? Things were definitely a bit weird today.

"Come on, Hughie," Gran said, "Let's get you into some dry clothes."

"The beaver's gone," Grandad pointed out. Then, with a twinkle, he added, "We told that beaver he couldn't log around here."

"Yeh," the wet child said with a frown. "So maybe he's in jail now."

His grandfather tousled his wet curls. "More likely they just put him back where he should have been all along, in Beaver Lake."

"Yeh!" Hughie accepted that with a decibel level that raised only one duck.

"Come on, dear," Gran urged, hustling him off toward home.

"Okay." Turning off the trauma like an off-switch, he scampered along with his grandmother while his sister and grandfather followed at an ear-protecting distance.

Xandra loved being with Grandad. Maybe . . . maybe because his eyes were so like Dad's. Blue, with a humorous twinkle. She smiled up at him as she said, "I'll bet that old beaver just got lonesome for his family and waddled back home on his own." Though she had not meant it to sound sad, Grandad patted her shoulder as he agreed. He knew how she felt about some things.

They could hear Hughie still going on about the beaver. Then he stopped suddenly. "Hey, Gran. Did you ever be a beaver?" What Gran had been in her past lives was an unending source of questions from Hughie.

"Imagine Gran a beaver," Xandra joked. She

made beaver teeth and held up her fingered paws.

"That nonsense about former lives," Grandad said briskly. He wasn't as impatient about it as Mom, though.

Xandra shrugged with amusement at her grandmother's weird ideas. "You wouldn't catch me getting hypnotized."

"I should think not," he replied.

Eager to change the subject, Xandra said, "Know what, Grandad? Tomorrow Gran is taking me over to Granville Island."

"Well now. That's splendid."

He didn't know how splendid it was. He didn't know about the dream she had been building up around a certain girl she had seen the other time she had gone to Granville Island. The island was a wonderful place, always filled with people: grownups shopping in the market, little kids chasing pigeons out on the wharf, big kids dodging traffic on their way to the video games, families tossing coins to the one-man-band and girls jabbering together as they watched the boats go by along False Creek. It was a place where people could even hang out by themselves and not look lonely. But it was better to be with friends.

FRIENDS.

That was what she needed — a friend. Someone to go to the beach with. Even someone to watch the squirrels with so she wouldn't be lonely and imagine things, like being watched when there was no one around to watch her.

Everybody needed a friend. And Xandra had seen the girl she wanted for her friend.

Wind chimes!

She was in bed that night when it hit her — why she had been startled by that sudden tinkle at the pavilion.

Wind chimes had hung from a tree near the spot where Xandra had found Flora Lee's pendant. And it seemed that her playmate's sudden appearance in the deep shadows had always been announced by a tinkle from those wind chimes. And that was what the tinkle at the pavilion had touched, away down in Xandra's subconscious.

It had been a pretty strange day. First, that feeling that someone was watching her . . . then thoughts of Flora Lee coming on so strongly after all these years . . . and then Hughie insisting that he'd been pushed when there'd been nobody around but her.

Xandra plopped a pillow over her head and stifled a groan.

I was pushed.

It was the middle of the night when she wakened from a haunting rerun of those words: *I was pushed . . . I was pushed . . .*

She sat bolt upright in bed, replaying a scene from back in her childhood:

She had been standing in the dark at the top of the stairs, a little kid listening to her parents talking downstairs.

"But Connal," her mom was saying to her dad, "It's positively spooky, that business about Flora Lee."

"Ellen," Dad sounded pleasant, even playful. "Her Flora Lee is just a plain, ordinary, everyday invisible playmate."

"But what she needs is a plain, ordinary, everyday VISIBLE playmate."

And that was when Mom had brought in Jenny — Jenny with the careful curls and the frilly white pinafore over her pink dress and panties. But Xandra and Flora Lee had not wanted Jenny around, spoiling their fun. So Flora Lee had pushed Jenny into the creek at the bottom of the garden. And the screeches had brought Mom charging over the grass like a knight to the rescue. "Jenny," she had cried out as she'd swooped up the wet child. "What happened?"

"I was pushed in," Jenny had sniffed between sobs, and looked at Xandra.

"I didn't push her, Mom," she had pointed out, rather anxiously. Even at four she had been smart enough to know that it wouldn't be a good idea to snitch on Flora Lee and incur the wrath of two people who were bigger than she was.

Mom had looked down at her with narrowed eyes. "Alexandra?"

"Mom, I didn't push her."

"Well. I was pushed," Jenny had shouted, forgetting to cry.

And now, sitting bolt upright in bed all these years later, a terrible realization hit the girl who had had an invisible playmate.

She had told herself that it was Flora Lee who had pushed Jenny. But there hadn't been any Flora Lee. So it was Xandra herself who had done the pushing, then lied to Mom about it.

Flora Lee had been someone her imagination had conjured up to play with. She had also been someone to blame things on — things she herself had done. Like pushing Jenny into the creek. And it was guilt about the fact that had made her block out all thought of Flora Lee for years and years.

It was only seeing that pendant again after all those years that had started stirring up old memories, then finally brought them flooding back today.

The pendant.

From the moment she had first found it back there on the rock shelf, Xandra had sensed that it carried some kind of magic. It just had not occurred to a four-year-old that it might also carry trouble for someone who stole it. It was just a decorated bit of clear plastic.

Xandra plopped a pillow over her head to stifle a groan. A weird idea was something she could do without at the moment. And the knowledge that she had been a sneaky little kid.

Thank goodness she was going over to Granville Island tomorrow morning — Granville Island where she would see that ferry girl again and maybe talk to her. She sighed a long, lonely sigh. Then she deliberately tried to work up the scene of talking with that girl: *She'll say this . . . I'll say that . . .*

Somehow, though, her overworked imagination seemed to be suffering from burnout.

If only tomorrow would hurry up and get here!

THREE

The morning was as fresh as a daffodil. And a dream fisherman seemed to have gathered in all the stars of a summer night, then flung his net out on the sea. It was sparkling, alive.

As Xandra and her grandmother set off along the seawall walk to the little ferry dock, a breeze was ballooning a sailboat's red-white-and-blue spinnaker out on English Bay; and the sun was brightening several other white sailboats skimming over the water. The girl's spirits rose like a spiralling sea gull riding a lifting thermal.

It really was wonderful, living right by the sea, and especially by the Pacific Ocean with all the coast mountains misted blue by the distance and the nearer trees and grasses kept green by summer showers.

Xandra just knew that — somehow — she was going to get to know that girl she had spotted on the Granville Island ferry. Since Gran had come up with an idea for a book set on the island, she was sure to be going there often. And why not by ferry? Xandra's rising hopes were tied to that little passenger ferry.

She had seen it when they had gone to Granville Island before, by car, over the bridge. A small white fibreglass boat that shuttled across False Creek (a slender arm of the sea poking in from English Bay), the ferry had a scallop-edged awning that fluttered in every breeze, making you think of the old song "The Surrey with the Fringe on Top."

She had seen the girl when she had gone to the dock where the ferries landed their passengers. The girl had leapt lightly out of the boat, pulled it close to the dock and whipped its line around the cleat before holding the light craft steady as the three passengers clambered out. She was a Norse heroine with shiny pale braids, her feet firmly apart. A Viking girl in a school play. She had looked adventurous . . . daring.

"Let's go by the ferry next time," Xandra had urged her grandmother.

Now they were going. And there was the little ferry purring into its own dock.

And there was the girl.

This time, though, the girl was into a different role. Above cut-offs, she was wearing one of those huge white T-shirts with the black Haida design Xandra had drooled over in the museum gift shop, the one with a leaping killer whale, with its high dorsal fin sticking straight up, and a whipping tail and big gnashing teeth. She looked as lordly as the Haida canoeists in the picture Xandra had seen also at the museum. *Lords of the Coast*, the caption called them. She was everything Xandra would like to have been as she confidently leapt out, tied up and held the boat steady as the passengers got off.

Mom would sure approve of a friend as practical as that — a friend who was probably good at math and science. Instead of just following dreams. There wasn't much security in dreams.

But Dad had said: *A dream can come true if you dream it joyously enough. And keep your fingers crossed.* So what if it didn't seem to have worked for him? Just give him time. And the right part in a smash hit play.

Smiling brightly and crossing her fingers, Xandra walked briskly along the float, out to the ferry dock, where an old couple and a teenage boy were already waiting. The boy was clutching a notebook and constantly pushing up his thick-lensed glasses. They were joined by a tall woman in a khaki shirt with a lot of pockets and a tent-like khaki skirt; she was carrying a sketchbook. Maybe a student at the art school on Granville Island.

"This is nice," Gran said, greeting everyone with an encompassing wave of her gauzy purple sleeve.

The ferry girl gave her a bright smile. She gave all the passengers a bright smile — even the boy who seemed to be a bit of a geek.

Xandra loved the ferry's shining white hull, its flutter-edged blue awning and the red life jackets netted under the awning, no doubt enough for the ten or so people who could fit onto the bench seats along the sides of the boat.

"Okay, Hilary," the big blond ferryman called out to the girl as he switched on his electric motor. "Cast off."

"Right, Dad," the girl called back, shoving off with one foot as she stepped into the boat. "That'll be seventy-five cents each," she told the passengers, reaching to collect the fares as the blond man nosed the ferry out into the bay.

They looked completely at ease. Father and daughter, Xandra thought, suppressing an envious sigh.

And then the girl sat down beside her. "Is this your first trip on the ferry?" she asked in that free-and-easy way she had.

"Yes," Xandra rushed on. "But I've been to the Island before." She had a wild wish that they were heading off all the way to China. But it was only a seven-minute run under the bridge and up False Creek.

The khaki-clad woman just had time for some quick sketching of the ferryman at the wheel before the ferry purred into its dock by the enormous public market. Even this early, people were thronging the wharf areas — people and pigeons and sea gulls — while, below them, reflections trembled in the shining, shape-shifting world of the water.

As though very polite about letting others out

first, Xandra managed to be the last one off the ferry.

"See you," the girl said; and a lift of her eyebrows made it almost a question.

"See you," Xandra answered, trying desperately to keep her cool. Maybe she was going to have a friend. The girl was busy now, but it would be easy to keep an eye on the ferry and just happen by when she seemed to have time on her hands, or when she left the boat to go and buy a muffin or fish-and-chips or something in the market.

As she watched the artist seat herself on a plank shelf and begin sketching, Xandra wished that she, too, had a good excuse to hang around.

She was following the others up the ramp when she heard the SPLASH and spun around.

"What happened?" the ferryman was asking his daughter as he reached down to give her a hand up out of the water. "You never fall in."

"I didn't fall in," she answered emphatically. "I was pushed!" Her eyes were snapping.

I was pushed. Xandra caught her breath. Held it for a moment. *I was pushed.* The words had an unnerving echo. Hughie had said them only yesterday, recalling Jenny's long-ago protest. She tried to shake off an eerie feeling. It was just a coincidence. Hughie had slipped on a muddy bank. The ferry girl had slipped on a wet dock. There was nothing eerie about it.

"I was pushed," the dripping girl insisted.

"Well, don't look at me," the ferryman said. "I didn't do it."

"Dad, somebody pushed me."

"But that's crazy — unless there's some remote

control going on from across there." He gestured
helplessly to the other side of the creek where they
were starting work on Expo 86, the World's Fair.
"You fell in, Hil. You'd better get changed." He made
a saluting gesture toward the interested spectators.
"She's okay," he said.

Clearly his daughter did not think so. "Dad!" Her
fists were belligerently on her hips now.

Xandra stayed part way up the ramp, staring back
for a few more moments. What was going on? People
being pushed when there was no one around to push
them. People being watched when there was no one
around to watch them. Her heart was thumping as
she stepped aside to let the dripping girl stomp angrily by. It was . . . creepy. WHAT was going on?

Xandra went up the ramp to the wharf area and
on into the market, though she scarcely noticed the
flower stalls and the fish counter, the piles and heap-
ing pyramids of oranges and potatoes, peaches and
broccoli. Anybody working around boats was bound
to fall in sooner or later. That girl had simply fallen
in and didn't like to admit it. The same as Hughie.

"So forget it," she mumbled to herself as she
waited by the strawberry stand while Gran was glancing around, probably making mental notes . . . maybe
about the guitarist by a side door.

Eager to recapture the happy mood her dad said
helped dreams to come true, Xandra watched him.
With his sign resting against the top of his open gui-
tar-case cash-receiver, he was singing "We're Off to
See the Wizard," and he was something to watch: red-
white-and-blue plaid pants, orange-white-and-green

plaid jacket with too short sleeves, and a yellow-and-black plaid cap.

She couldn't help smiling. She loved Granville Island. It was as sensible as potatoes, yet crazy as a clown.

"First, my cappuccino," Gran announced, heading for Dino's stall. "What shall I get for you?"

"Hot chocolate and muffin, please, Gran." They had scrumptious muffins at one stall, and Gran knew which one. "I'll look for a table."

Tables were hard to find. Gran wouldn't want one of those crowded ones under the yellow-and-orange-striped awning in the fast food area. She liked to sit outside or, better still, by the big windows where you could watch the sailboats go by, and the tugs and fishboats and motor cruisers, maybe even a racing shell filled with oarsmen. And that suited Xandra. There, she could keep an eye on that little ferry.

It was a glorious morning. She had met that girl, with every prospect of being friends. And there was a table, right by the window.

Yet . . .

"You're looking very thoughtful, dear," Gran remarked as Xandra was finishing her apple-and-raisin muffin.

"Well . . ." Maybe if she talked about it, she'd see how silly her feelings were.

"Well . . . what?" Gran urged her.

"Well . . ." Then again, maybe it wouldn't be such a good idea to talk about it . . . to put weird, disturbing thoughts into words as if . . .

"Tell me, dear," her grandmother coaxed. After all, she was writing kids' books, so she liked to know what kids thought about.

"Gran, Hughie said he was pushed into Lost Lagoon and I didn't do it. Really," Xandra said, taking the plunge. "And that girl on the ferry said she was pushed in, too, when there was no one around to push her, either. And . . ." She swallowed.

"Something else, Xandra?"

"No . . . well, . . . yes . . . maybe. Yesterday in the park, when I was playing with the squirrels, I just know that someone was watching me."

A worried look flickered across her grandmother's face. "Gran, it wasn't a mugger or something. It was . . ." She dropped her voice to a whisper. "It was . . . you know . . . kind of . . . spooky."

"Spooky?" Gran's voice, too, was a whisper. She didn't think people who had weird things happen to them were crazy.

"Well . . . hey!" Xandra said, glad to be interrupted, "There's the ferry coming in again." She had noticed that there were two little ferries to handle the morning shoppers. And though this was the one the girl worked on, she still was not on it.

Still changing her clothes somewhere, Xandra thought, wondering where. There were no houses near the market, apart from the houseboats in Sea Village beyond the art school. Sea Village had a wooden "street" with T-posts that held hanging baskets spilling with geraniums and ivy; it had houseboats with flowers cascading from their sun decks, and gleaming yachts moored alongside. But that would be too perfect if she lived there. Maybe the girl had sprinted all the way to those red-roofed condominiums farther along the creek.

"Think I'll walk around, Gran," Xandra announced as soon as she had eaten the last crumbs of her muffin. She felt too restless to sit there wondering if she was going to spot that girl again.

"Well, stay near the market," Gran stipulated. She had been fingering her notebook while her eyes took on that faraway look her granddaughter recognized. Now she dipped into her Mexican bag. "Would you get me another cappuccino before you wander off?"

"Cappuccino coming right up!" Xandra said as she took the three dollars. "Three?" Cappuccino cost just ninety-nine cents. "Thanks, Gran." She dashed off.

Gran needn't worry about her not staying near the market. It was out there, on its west wharf, that she was most likely to spot that girl heading back to the ferry. Xandra was dashing out through the flower shop exit when she heard the tinkle.

Wind chimes.

Oh no. Xandra stopped in dismay. Glancing up, she saw them, chimes, hanging from a beam with baskets of fuchsias on both sides. She felt a shiver go through her.

Don't be silly, she admonished herself. Wind chimes always tinkled, even in the slightest breeze. Only . . . there wasn't the slightest breeze in this sheltered area. The air was dead still.

But of course there was some explanation. Someone had brushed by, carrying a tall plant. Only there didn't seem to be anyone around with a tall plant. Not even a kid with a balloon. She hurried on, out onto the wharf, controlling a shudder.

Several times she had noticed the boy from the

ferry while she had been walking around the market
and while she had been eating her muffin. Now he
was hovering nearby like a friendly, hopeful puppy.
Well. She was not going to speak to him — not when
she had to be alone . . . to be free to sprint off if she
saw that girl coming. It was hard to stage an acciden-
tal meeting while someone was watching you.

Why didn't he go somewhere else?

It was his hopeful hovering that finally drove
Xandra back into the market. Anyway, she told herself, the girl would probably come from the other side,
from one of the condominiums, and go through the
market to pick up something to eat on her way back
to the ferry.

Xandra tried to be very unobtrusive about easing
herself back inside. She hoped to give those big eyes
behind the glasses the slip — like giving your "tail" the
slip in a spy drama.

It was a brief hope. There he was, only a few stalls
away.

Why didn't he buzz off?

She was strolling by some grapes and oranges and
raspberries, still carefully ignoring him, when a voice
said, "Hi," right behind her.

Xandra spun round, though nobody could be talking to her.

But somebody *was* talking to her. The girl from
the ferry, now in dry shorts and a T-shirt.

"Did you see anyone push me, after you got off?"
the girl asked; and her eyes seemed to be shooting
off blue sparks.

"No. But then I didn't look back until after I

heard the splash . . . Let me see now . . . " Actually, Xandra hadn't an idea in the world, except to keep this girl with her. "My grandmother and the rest of the passengers were up ahead of me on the ramp — except for the artist, of course. Hey. Maybe that artist saw something."

The ferry girl flashed her anger. "That woman said she was sketching my dad and not looking at me. So she didn't see anything, either. But somebody pushed me."

Xandra swallowed. "Did you . . . feel a hand?" she asked, nervously interested. Hughie too had said "I was pushed."

The girl narrowed her eyes. "You know . . . it was more like a . . . a blast of air, hitting me hard right behind the knees."

"A . . . blast? But there wasn't a sound or anything, was there?" Xandra caught her breath.

"No." Now looking more thoughtful than angry, the girl turned to leave. "I better get back."

"Do you work on the ferry?" A dumb question.

"Yeh. Sort of. My dad lets me do things. He's looking after me this summer."

"Oh." Xandra knew all about that. "And he lives in one of those condos?" she went on, gesturing vaguely eastward.

"No. One of the houseboats. They don't have kids living there, but I'm just visiting, sort of. And I don't hang around much." For one flick of time, the Norse heroine looked as wistful as a waif.

"Living there at all!" Xandra squealed. "Wow. Imagine sitting out there on one of those flowery decks, watching the boats go by . . . Oh . . . uh . . . My name's

Xandra. Alexandra Warwick."

"Mine's Hilary. Hilary Olsen." She turned to leave, slipped on something, grabbed wildly to save herself, and sent a pile of oranges tumbling across the floor, surprising the people around the fruit stand.

"Hey. What happened?" Xandra asked as she squatted down to help pick up the scattered fruit. "Was it a banana peel?" she asked, glancing about. But there wasn't a banana peel anywhere, not a squashed grape or raspberry, nor even a wet leaf of lettuce. She could feel her heart thumping.

"That's what I'd like to know." Hilary's smouldering anger flared up. "Something weird's going on around here. And I want to know what it is." She had her fists on her hips again. "It felt more like . . . like I was tripped."

"Tripped?" But everyone had been at least an arm's length away from her. Xandra swallowed.

What *was* going on?

And how would anyone . . . anything . . . dare to tackle Hilary?

FOUR

"Did you happen to think of a poltergeist?" the boy from the ferry asked, barging into their conversation. He started to flick through the notebook that Xandra had noticed him carrying earlier. "Here it is. 'Poltergeist. A boisterous spirit.'"

"Spirit!" While the word burst out from Hilary as an explosion of disbelief, like a shot from a gun, Xandra's word came out more like the fizzle of a wet firecracker. Things were bad enough already without this boy talking about spirits. But he would know about something like poltergeists.

He was considering his poltergeist notes with a frown. "They usually throw things or shake things or set fires," he informed the girls. "I don't think they make people slip or push them into the sea. But they might." His face brightened. "Sure they might." He frowned again before he looked straight at Xandra. "Are you a disturbed adolescent?"

"A what? No, I'm not," she snapped as she plunked the last orange into the pile. What did a disturbed adolescent have to do with anything anyway? "I'm not a disturbed anything." Of all the dumb ideas.

"Are you?" Hilary asked the boy, sizing him up, her eyes narrowed. Her tone might have stopped a grizzly.

"Me? Oh no," he smiled tentatively as he ducked his head to adjust his glasses.

"You could be," Hilary went on in a none-too-friendly manner.

Yes, you could be, Xandra silently agreed. She noticed his name on his notebook. Holbridge Herkins. A name like that was enough to make you into an anything.

"Do you live around here?" Hilary sure was direct with people. And a little blunt. She assumed command.

"No. I'm just visiting my aunt for a month."

"Well, maybe you better go home to your aunt. Poltergeist," Hilary snorted. She glared at the boy. Then she turned narrowed eyes on Xandra. "Maybe you *are* a disturbed adolescent." And she glanced sharply at the floor before she strode off.

Gone. Without even a friendly, "See you."

Xandra controlled the theatrical despair she was tempted to let overcome her. "And I've got to get back to my grandmother," she lied, to escape from the boy. She had had enough of him and his notebook. He had ruined her chance to make a friend. She turned and rushed off blindly, almost hitting someone — the artist. She muttered a fast "sorry" and hurried on.

Crazy things were happening. Too many crazy things. She pushed down a mounting panic as she neared her grandmother.

"Am I a disturbed adolescent?" she gasped out as she flung herself into the chair.

"At this moment I'd say yes, dear." Gran looked somewhat surprised by the question, but her voice was soothingly quiet. "Xandra, what happened?"

"You tell me," Xandra begged, lowering her voice as she caught glances from the family eating fish and chips at a nearby table. "Gran, what's a poltergeist?"

"Poltergeist?" Gran seemed quite relieved by the question. "Well . . . " she went on, "sometimes mysterious things start happening — things being hurled about when apparently no one has touched them. And —"

"That's what a poltergeist does," Xandra broke in. "But what is it? A ghost or something?"

"Probably . . ." Gran smiled as if ghosts were as natural as squirrels and about as threatening. "A poltergeist seems to be an annoyed spirit-being that is getting a lot of help from a disturbed adolescent."

"Well! I'm not a disturbed adolescent." She couldn't be . . . Could she? She hadn't tripped Hilary.

"You certainly are not," Gran said spiritedly. "What happened? Why did you ask about a poltergeist?"

"Well . . . That's what that boy said it was when

Hilary slipped. On NOTHING."

"Hilary?"

"The ferry girl. She said she was pushed on the dock. Then she said she was tripped in the market. That's two things that happened to her this morning, with no one around to make them happen. I know they happened. I was there. Both times."

Xandra's hand flew to her mouth. *I was there. Both times.*

Could she be a disturbed adolescent? Helping a . . . ? No. The thought made her shudder.

Though her grandmother's eyes had widened for a moment, now they were part of a smile. "I wouldn't worry about it, dear. You're not disturbed." She went on talking about poltergeists as if Xandra had brought up a delightful subject. "They may do some annoying things," she commented. "But they never seem to actually harm anyone."

Xandra opened her mouth. Closed it. She slumped down in her chair. It wasn't having anyone harmed that was worrying her. It was just the whole idea of people being pushed and tripped . . . of that stupid boy bringing up poltergeists and disturbed adolescents, making Hilary think that maybe she — Xandra — was a weirdo, a . . . a poltergeist's pal. Driving Hilary away. Hilary. Her one hope for a summer friend. "Gran, you don't really believe in things like poltergeists?" Her eyes begged her grandmother to say no.

"Well . . . Why not? These mysterious things do seem to happen. So there has to be something making them happen. And if we can't see what it is, it must be an invisible something. A spirit being, perhaps . . . a poltergeist."

"But . . . but what about the disturbed adolescent?"

"Well, as I understand it, dear, to do physical things — like throwing a clock across a room, say — a spirit has to draw energy from a person; and if there happens to be an angry young person who would like to throw that clock across the room, the poltergeist has a ready source of power."

"But . . . but . . . but . . . " Xandra's squawk was like a clucky old hen's. "But does that person know she's helping to throw the clock?"

"Probably not, though she may sense that something is happening. Seems that when energy is drawn from a person, that person feels a strangeness." She put a hand over her solar plexus. "An emptiness. A sense of being drained."

Emptiness! She had felt an emptiness in the park; and it may not have been just from skipping breakfast. It had hit her like a hurled clock. But she couldn't be a poltergeist's energizer. She couldn't help do things that would drive Hilary away. She couldn't!

A flash of anger came to her rescue. Anger against Gran. Just because she believed all those crazy things . . . just because she did crazy things — all in the interests of researching a story, of course — Gran thought that other people should believe in all those crazy things, too. Look at the crazy things she did — like getting hypnotized to find out about the other lives she had lived before this one. Of all the loony things for a grandmother to do!

Yet . . .

Maybe she, Xandra, *was* a disturbed adolescent. People said that kids could get disturbed when their parents split. Well maybe she was disturbed. But not *that* disturbed. She hadn't been powering a poltergeist at Lost Lagoon to help push Hughie in.

And Hilary? No way. She had so wanted Hilary to like her, to stay talking with her. So she couldn't have made her slip, on the dock or in the market.

It seemed ages before they went home — by bus because she simply could not face Hilary. "I'm not going over to Granville Island with you next time," she said while they were walking home from the bus. If she had to have a friend, maybe she could get hypnotized back to ancient Egypt and find one. "What's it like when you're drifted back to a past life?" Not that she believed there was a past life to be drifted back to. "What's . . . what's it like?"

"Oh, I find it fascinating. It's a bit like watching a story unfold on a screen."

"You mean . . . ? You see somebody else doing it?"

"Yes. And no. In one session I watched a girl going west in a covered wagon. I saw her as if she were somebody else; yet, when they were attacked and she fell off, I saw the next wagon going over *me*. I was on the ground, looking up at it."

"Weird." Xandra hunched her shoulders in distaste. She didn't really believe her grandmother. But one thing did cheer her. "So it *is* like seeing a story unfold on a screen. It's like *you* getting into a scene you could write about."

"Well, yes. And I do make up stories, don't I?"

Gran dismissed the subject with an airy wave. "No one can know for sure about past lives."

Or about poltergeists. And all those screwy ideas were going to make her a disturbed adolescent if she wasn't one already.

At least she had enough sense not to bring up the subject later, when she was stacking the dishwasher after the soup and sandwich supper she had set out. Her mother looked distraught enough as it was.

"I'll be working 'til midnight," Mom groaned as she thumped her briefcase down on the cleared table. "That man sets impossible deadlines. All this on his desk at eight a.m. tomorrow. Completely unrealistic." Even in a bright turquoise sweat suit, she looked as if she had just been dragged in from a tough hour on a rock pile.

"Tell him to stuff it, Mom."

"How I wish I could. But it's a smile-if-it-kills-you world out there, Xandra. Once your income gets up to an acceptable level, a lot of men want your job; they're lining up to leap in the moment you can't hack it." Her mother narrowed her eyes on the big sheaf of papers she was lifting out of the briefcase. "It's getting better, but women still have to try harder."

"Well, I'll get Hughie to bed, Mom, after I read him his story."

"I should be doing that." Her mother sighed a deep sigh. But she had to pay the rent and make sure the kids went to college. She opened her mouth again

to make an angry remark. Then shut it. She furiously
tackled the sheaf of papers. Thank goodness. Xandra
did not want to hear something that might make her
even more of a disturbed adolescent than she already
was. And Hughie was squawking for his story.

Xandra had loved it when Dad had read to
Hughie, and to her. Using his trained voice, he had
made things shiveringly scary or roll-on-the-floor
funny. Why hadn't he stayed with them? In spite of
the fights about money?

They leave you.

Flora Lee had been right about that. But there
was no Flora Lee. And it was sick to think about an
imaginary playmate as if she had been a real girl.

Hughie was making impatient noises from the
couch.

"Quiet," she ordered in a loud whisper, indicating
their mother at work. Actually, she enjoyed reading
to Hughie. His kind of stories gave her lots of scope
for being dramatic. And he was a great audience, by
turns excited, anxious, scared stiff or jubilant, no matter how many times he had heard the story. No
wonder Dad had joined a children's theatre group
that wandered the highways and byways in colourful
vans. *The Canada Goose Storytellers* played in school
gyms and community centres. It was not a great way
to help your family buy a car that didn't break down
all the time. But the shows were pure magic.

Xandra blinked back her tears to get on with
Hughie's story about the poor fisherman who had
cast his net into the sea only to draw in a dead jack-
ass, then a basketful of sand and mud, then nothing

but stones and shell and rubbish and then . . . "Then," she went on . . .

Put everything you've got into it! She could almost hear her father's voice, and her shoulders — now sagged with the poor man's dismay at all his bad luck — lifted as the next catch brought in an elegant urn, an urn that must hold precious treasure. Xandra was almost as breathless as the fisherman while he carefully broke the seal at the top, and her audience held his breath as a cloud of smoky vapour emerged from the vase and spread into an enormous thick fog that turned itself into a gigantic GENIE — a genie that threatened to kill the fisherman.

Hughie sat wide-eyed with anxiety as the terrified man tried to save himself by talking the genie back into the urn as he pretended to believe that the genie could not possibly have fitted into such a small vessel. "I shall not believe you unless I were to see it."

Hughie could no longer hold in his excitement. "So the silly genie be'd a fog again and slipped back into the urn." Then he almost held his breath until the urn was safely sealed and flung back into the sea.

"That's all for tonight," Xandra declared as she closed the book.

"But there's more," Hughie protested.

"Not tonight," his sister informed him as she dragged him off to the bathroom. "Time to throw YOU into the water," she warned, since his idea of a good wash was to wet one finger and streak it across his neck.

When Hughie had been settled into bed, Xandra took *The Secret Garden* to the couch; the TV would disturb Mom while she was working. But tonight she didn't seem to settle into the story. She kept thinking about that poltergeist thing. She wasn't a poltergeist's pal. But she couldn't stop thinking about it.

When she went to her room later, she lifted Gopo off the bed. A clown puppet with a stretchy face, he had been a gift from her father. "Gopo. I am not a poltergeist's energizer," she told him as she made him scowl. Then she laid him on the chest of drawers near her photograph of Dad.

"Something weird is going on, Dad," she whispered to the picture. "And it isn't me." Then, with a long, lonely sigh, she took her lacquered treasure chest out of the top drawer. She was blinking back tears even before she started going through her treasures.

First there was the picture-wallet the four girls at her farewell party had given her, with snapshots of each of the four — crazy snapshots. Once she had had four good friends. Xandra wiped a splash off one of the snapshots.

Then she held the tie close — the blue-and-brown striped tie Dad had overlooked when he had taken his things. Stroking its silky smoothness, she remembered how it had made his blue eyes even bluer.

Why did things have to change?

She smiled wistfully at the happy pictures in the little album that recorded her birthdays. Every one showed Dad doing that year's act with her, the birthday girl; while Mom was happily watching.

Everything had been so wonderful. Once.

She took the pendant out of her hip pocket. Maybe she should put it in with the other keepsakes. But no. It was beautiful and she was going to wear it. So, after running a finger over its glassy smoothness, she laid it on the chest of drawers, right beside Gopo.

That night it seemed hours before she went to sleep, weeping about her lovely, lost years. And it was the sound of weeping that pulled her out of a troubled sleep sometime about the middle of the night.

But not her own weeping.

Peering, half asleep, around her dark room, she found the source of the weeping — a small, huddled figure on the floor by the chest of drawers, near the end where she had put Gopo.

"Hughie?" But she knew it was not her small brother. That was a small girl figure over there, holding something in her arms, weeping as if her heart was breaking. Xandra couldn't move.

Suddenly the weeping stopped.

The huddled figure vanished.

As if it had never been, the huddled figure vanished.

It was just her imagination. It had never been there. Xandra yanked the covers over her head, and tried to control her shivering.

What on earth was happening to her?

What was happening to a world that had once been so safe and warm?

And WHY was it happening?

FIVE

The usual sudden blast of music on her mother's radio woke Xandra to a gorgeous summer day with the sea breezes billowing her curtains.

Scarcely remembering why, she glanced down at the corner of the room near the chest of drawers. The sight of her puppet on the floor brought it all flooding back: the weeping . . . the small huddled figure . . . the sudden vanishing into thin air. She had been dreaming, of course. But —

But Gopo was on the floor! And she had put him

on top of the chest of drawers, near her father's picture. So the wind came up during the night, blew the curtains in harder, and the curtains swept the puppet off that slippery-smooth wood. That was all there was to it. So she hopped out of bed to put him back where he should be, and —

And that was when she saw the pendant, down there on the floor with Gopo.

The pendant!

So what? When the curtain had swept the puppet off, the puppet had swept the pendant off. So why did she find herself shivering a little?

Why?

Because she was a disturbed adolescent with a totally terrible imagination that she was going to control. As of this morning, she, Alexandra Warwick, was going to take things in hand.

It was like the story of the poor fisherman and the genie. Worries about the mysterious happenings had spread around her like the vapour from the copper urn; and this vapour, too, had turned into a genie that was threatening to kill her. Well, not kill her exactly. Just spoil her life. But was she going to stand there cowering? Or was she going to take charge of the situation the way the fisherman had? And get that amorphous monster back into the urn and hurl the whole thing out into the sea?

The fisherman had talked his way out of his dilemma, hadn't he? So for starters, Xandra was going to talk to Hilary. Straight, strong talk, not that silly dithering squeak she usually came out with. Today she was abandoning the role of mouse. Today she was an eagle. A tiger. A whatever it took.

"Hi, Mom," she said as she strode into the coffee-fragrant kitchen. "All set to knock 'em dead with all the work you got done?" She added an encouraging hug. Mom, too, had her problems.

"I'll knock 'em dead," her mother answered, as brightly as possible, considering a shortage of sleep. "Xandra, you will see that Hughie eats breakfast before you take him to daycare?"

"Yep. Fruit and mush and ham and eggs and a steak with hash-browns. He'll need strength for that beaver hunt. Grandad's going to help him track down that four-footed vandal with the big teeth."

"I don't know what we'd do without Grandad," her mother said.

Or Gran. Now Xandra remembered that she had told her grandmother she was not going back to Granville Island. But that was before she'd become an eagle. As soon as her mother had dashed off with her briefcase, Xandra got on the phone. "Gran, if you're going back to Granville Island today, I really would like to go with you. I . . . You see, I have a pendant that I found in the rock garden at our old house and I need to buy a chain so I can wear it. I still have the money you gave me." Now why did she bring up the pendant? Why? Clearly lacking the poor fisherman's cool, she always jumped in and rattled off the first thing that came to her mind. Nervous reaction or something. And now she was stuck with the pendant.

"I was planning on working this morning and going over there right after lunch," Gran told her. "And I'd love to have you with me."

After Xandra had walked Hughie to daycare and had tidied up the apartment, she took a book down to the beach where there were lots of people around. She bought a hamburger for lunch. And by one-thirty, she and Gran were once more hiking along the seawall walk toward the little ferry dock at Sunset Beach. To support her explanation to Gran, she had the pendant in her small shoulder bag. There were lots of craft places where she could look for a chain.

Gran sure loved the colour purple. Today her purple panty hose matched the wild purple pattern in her pink dress. At least — thank goodness — she did not put a purple rinse on her short silvery hair. Actually she was a classy lady, in an arty way. Xandra admired her even if she did do some pretty far out things. "Gran, I'd love to have Hilary for a friend," she said as she laid an appealing hand on a fluttery sleeve. "She's awfully nice."

"If a bit accident prone," her grandmother agreed.

"Well, I sure hope she doesn't have any more accidents near me." That falling and slipping had just happened. It could happen to anyone, anywhere; and sometimes it just happened to happen all at once. That was what she was going to point out to Hilary.

While she was at it, she might as well say something to Gran too. Point blank. She took a deep breath and said it. "Gran, I am not a poltergeist's source of power."

"I know that, dear."

Surprised by the positive answer, Xandra came out with, "What do you mean — you know that?"

"Well, let's just say I have a sort of sixth sense

about things. Psi power."

"Like those people the police call in to tell them where the stolen ring is, or the missing body?"

"Well, not that exactly. But I do know that you are not the kind of angry young person a poltergeist looks for."

Xandra heaved a sigh of relief before she asked, "Gran, can you bend spoons with your mind?"

"I haven't tried bending spoons." Gran laughed it off with a gesture that her granddaughter interpreted as *I think I could if I put my mind to it*. Then pointing ahead to the ferry dock, she said, "It's a gorgeous day for a sea voyage."

It was a gorgeous day. The beach thronged with sunbathers and the bay was full of sails. And now, with her decision that she was not a poltergeist's pal confirmed by Gran, Xandra's spirits lifted like a helium balloon. She felt the old stirring of excitement about Granville Island. It was such a crazy mixup of fish and flowers, yachts and tugboats, cement-mixer yards and artists' studios, people and pigeons, with the big arches of the bridge overhead and the city out there beyond them. It was a stage set. But would it be a happy ending on her stage? Would it be a successful run for *Xandra Gets a Friend*?

"Oh, no," she murmured as they neared the dock. "There's Holbridge Herkins again." He stirred on his driftwood log when he saw them, and closed his notebook. Darn. How was she ever going to get anywhere with Hilary while he was hovering around, listening in and barging into their conversation?

Then she saw Hilary coming in on the ferry, with

a new glint above her shorts and T-shirt. Silver earrings, she saw as the little ferry came into its dock.
Gorgeous Haida earrings. Like Mom had pointed out
to her in the museum gift shop. "Wow," she breathed
in absolute awe. Mom would kill for earrings like that.

But Mom's daughter took things in hand. She sang
out, "Hi, Hilary. Any more dunkings or trippings?"
Those accidents had nothing to do with Alexandra
Warwick, and she was not going to act as if they had.

Hilary grinned. "It was just my bad day, I guess."
She jerked her head toward the boy now on the dock.
"He's been hanging around for about an hour. I
think he was waiting for you." Her silver earrings
flashed as she turned to grin at Xandra.

They both hunched their shoulders in a quick gig-
gle. Too relieved to think of acting cool, Xandra
relaxed into Hilary's free-and-easy attitude about the
events of that day. She could just be what she wanted
to be — a girl with a friend.

"Hi." The boy's face was one big wide smile as he
climbed awkwardly aboard the blue-awninged ferry,
making it rock.

"Hi." Both girls greeted him without enthusiasm.

"Can you get off for awhile?" Xandra asked when
the fare collecting was over and Hilary had slipped
down beside her.

"Sure. Dad doesn't mind, long as I check in now
and then. Tell you a secret." She raised her voice and
grinned at her father. "Dad *can* handle the boat without me." She returned his wink saucily.

Hilary was so GREAT.

When they docked, Hilary waved to the khaki-clad

woman who was now sitting up on the wharf, eyes moving back and forth between the sea and the sketchbook. "Is she always over here?" Xandra asked.

"Just about every day. And she always wears the same clothes," Hilary whispered. They giggled. FRIENDS.

After all Xandra's fears of being rebuffed, there had been nothing to it. Like the fisherman, she had handled the situation. Her troubles were over. And she could have hugged herself.

She could have done a handstand, right there on the ramp.

She could have taken off like a helium balloon. Her troubles were over.

Gran said she was going to have her cappuccino up in the loft area, where there was a great view, not only of the boats going by, but also of everything that was happening down below at that end of the market, where the fast food stalls and the tables shared space with fish and farm produce.

"Maybe we could take something out on the wharf, Gran," Xandra hoped.

"Of course. Tell me what you'd like."

"Couldn't we just roam around and see what we'd like?" the granddaughter countered. "After you're settled."

"Fine." Gran dipped into her Mexican hold-all and gave Xandra a five dollar bill. "Here's some money for food and a little more for that chain you mentioned you wanted to buy. Try to get me a table by the railing, Xandra." She moved off toward Dino's stall.

"What chain?" Hilary was brightly interested.

"Oh . . . one to suit this." Xandra resolutely opened her shoulder bag as they went up the stairs to the loft to find a table for Gran.

"Neat," Hilary said as she took the pendant and began sliding her fingers over it, delighting in the painted-on flowers: wild roses, forget-me-nots, violets, bluebells, all swirling mistily together with green vines under a glassy glaze. "Let's get a chain for it right away so you can wear it."

Half an hour later, Xandra was wearing the pendant while they were getting themselves all sticky with Greek baklava out on the east wharf.

"I like your grandmother," Hilary remarked.

"She's great." No way was Xandra going to say anything that might dim her own image in her friend's eyes. She was resolutely having as much fun as Hilary was, watching a couple of boys paddle by in kayaks, and she was keeping her fingers crossed about Holbridge Herkins, now hovering near an outdoor fruit stand, watching them and glancing at his ever-present notebook. Didn't he have anything else to do?

When Hilary suggested getting a drink, Xandra whispered, "And give him the slip?"

Giggling over their conspiracy, they waited until he had turned to buy something from the fruit stand. Then dashed into the market.

As they stood in line waiting for their fresh melon juice, Xandra glanced up at the coffee loft. Gran was sitting by the rail, gazing down through those funny little binoculars she had bought by mail order from Florida. "Micro-mini-spy-glasses," she had called them. "They help me to concentrate." Well, she certainly seemed to be concentrating on something right now.

For no reason she could think of, Xandra felt a

sudden chill along her spine. Like when she was being watched in the park. Oh, no! Something weird was not going to happen again? Not now, just when things were going so great. "I think they must be growing the melons," she whispered to Hilary. And when she found herself fingering the pendant, she snatched her hand away, as if from a live wire. Smarten up, she silently ordered herself. A pendant was just a pendant. It was nothing but plastic and painted-on flowers.

Gran was still staring down through those glasses. What on earth was she looking at?

"What's your gran looking at?" Hilary echoed her thoughts as they finally moved off with their melon juice.

"Who knows?" Xandra answered lightly, though her heart had started thumping with apprehension. "Gran writes children's books. Far out fantasies sometimes. She's working on a story now with this setting."

"Wow." Hilary was impressed. "I noticed she wears purple pantyhose."

"Well, you know . . . writers." Xandra waved her free hand to encompass any loony things writers might do.

"Wow." Hilary said again. So Gran's peculiarities might actually win points with this friend, who whispered, "Hey, look. I don't think we've lost him." H.H., as they'd dubbed him, was heading their way from the big fish market in the corner. "Let's go to the houseboat. He can't follow us there."

"Okay. Let's go." It was Xandra's turn to be impressed. *Houseboat*!

They were moving off toward the side door when the small fish hit Hilary, right on one dangling killer whale earring.

"Hey!" Hilary exploded.

Xandra gasped, staring down at the dead fish on the floor. The back of her neck was prickling, and a spot under the pendant felt peculiar. But it couldn't be. It couldn't!

She glanced wildly about. H.H. was standing near the fish stall, staring at them with his mouth open. He couldn't have done it. She glanced at the fish stall. Two older women were there, picking out what they wanted. And they wouldn't throw a fish. The khaki-clad artist was there, just behind H.H. glancing alertly around.

"Who threw that fish at me?" Hilary demanded, standing in spilled juice with her free fist belligerently on her hip. Ready to slaughter whoever did.

Gran's words echoed somewhere in Xandra's head: *things being hurled about when apparently no one has touched them.* No! A real person could have thrown that fish.

"Did you happen to think of psychokinesis?" H.H. asked as he closed in on them, eyes on his open notebook. "You know, things being moved by the power of someone's mind in fierce concentration."

"Who would do a thing like that?" Xandra shrilled. She was still pushing down a rising alarm about being a poltergeist's pal after all, when she looked up towards the coffee loft. Her grandmother was scanning the room with her binoculars. And the sense of what H.H. had said hit her: *things being moved by the power of someone's mind in fierce concentration. . . .* Gran's mind? Its power concentrated by those micro-mini-spy-glasses? Could *she* have hurled that fish? Just to prove that some silly old character in her story could hurl a fish by . . . by whatever H.H. had said?

Then she noticed that Hilary was looking at her — Xandra — the way she might look at the person who had pushed her into the water. "It always happens when I'm with you," she stated. "Only when I'm with YOU, Alexandra Warwick."

"But . . . but . . . but . . . but he was around, too," Xandra protested, grabbing wildly at any defence.

H.H. was too busy flipping through his notebook to be offended. "Psychokinesis," he burst out as he jabbed a finger down on a page. "Psi phenomenon. Things moved by the conscious power of someone's mind. The conscious power of someone's mind," H.H. repeated, almost crowing his revelation.

"How'd you like the conscious power of someone's fist?" Hilary challenged him, raising her own fist. "I'm going back to the boat. I don't like what's happened since I met you two." She strode off.

Gone. Gone for ever.

"I think it is psychokinesis," the boy said, beaming at Xandra. "Psi power."

"Oh, go jump in a fish tank," she snapped. Then she jostled her way through the crowd, making a bee-line for her grandmother.

"Psi power," she snorted. "Moving things by the power of the mind." Okay! If Gran had anything to do with that fish, she could just own up. Her anger against H.H. was now turned fully against the lady with the spy-glasses.

She was too mad to even notice the way her skin prickled under the pendant.

SIX

It had to be Gran and her research for the story that was making these weird things happen.

"Did you see that?" Xandra demanded as she plunked herself down at her grandmother's table in the coffee loft. "Hilary got hit on the ear by a fish — a fish that nobody threw! And she said things like that happen to her only since she met ME." She blinked back angry tears as she glared at her grandmother.

"Well, maybe that's true," Gran pointed out, as if she were pointing out that pigeons did seem to take startled flight only when they were near small children. "But strange coincidences happen, too."

Strange coincidences. Like GRAN always being around, too. And she would do anything to be sure about things for her dumb old stories. She had thrown that fish by psychokinesis, by the power of her mind in fierce concentration through those spyglasses. Xandra was willing to believe anything. Her grandmother had thrown that fish just to prove that psychokinesis would work for a character in her story.

Xandra opened her mouth to say exactly that. Then she clamped it shut. When it came right down to it, she could not — point blank — accuse her own grandmother of deliberately spoiling her life. She couldn't *say* Gran was that mean even if she was. So she slumped down in total misery. Hilary would never be her friend again.

"Can we go home by bus?" she asked. No way was she going to face Hilary again.

"Of course we can go home by bus," Gran agreed as she stowed her notebook. "Actually, I think I've done enough for today, dear."

I'll say you've done enough for today, Xandra silently stormed, even as she sensed that she wanted to keep something else — and she didn't know what the something else was — away deep down in her subconscious. But Gran's research craziness was part of whatever was going on, she was sure of that. She jumped up. Made for the stairs. Then headed for the exit.

WIND CHIMES.

She had forgotten that this was that exit.

Wind chimes. Like a tinkling reminder that it

might not be Gran who was doing the weird things.

But why shouldn't wind chimes tinkle? That's what they were there for, wasn't it? They had nothing to do with anybody's long-ago invisible playmate. Xandra angrily fingered the new chain and its pendant. Nothing had gone right since she had taken that pendant away from its hiding place. Xandra broke the new chain with a fierce tug. And as she went by the potted plant section, she let the necklace slip out of her fingers.

"We might miss the next bus," she called back to her grandmother as she sprinted off toward the bus stop. Free of the pendant.

Gran, as well as Xandra, was unusually quiet nearly all the way back by bus. Then, when they were walking along the seawall, she turned suddenly toward Xandra and put a hand on her shoulder. "Once when I visited you, dear, when you were about four, you had an invisible playmate. You could see her and hear her."

"Not really," Xandra countered, none too politely. She was surprised by Gran's remembering Flora Lee. But she was not going to be the object of any more research. "You know I like to pretend and act. Well, I was just pretending and acting then. Just making it all up." She put on her most theatrical bored expression.

Which Gran ignored. "You may not have been just making it all up. What is it St. Paul said about the gifts of the spirit? That some are given the gift of healing ... or ... the gift of prophecy ... or ... the gift of discerning spirits. Of being able to see spirit beings."

Of being able to see spirit beings? That was in the Bible? Xandra's uneasy anger flared up again. Gran was just up to her old tricks. Maybe she had an invisible playmate in that story she was researching, as well as a character with psi power. And if she had, she could just go and do her research on somebody else.

"I don't think I'll bother going over to Granville Island again," Xandra managed a yawn. "It gets boring."

Her whole lovely friendship had ended with a dead fish; and that happening was not just a coincidence, just something that happened to happen. Somebody was doing something weird; and what was that somebody — or something — going to do next? These things all happened to Hilary, yet . . . it was all happening to her, Xandra, to her dreams of having Hilary as a friend.

Xandra's sigh could have ruffled the sea if the sea had been a little closer. After all her high spiralling hopes, the rest of the summer stretched out ahead of her, endless and empty, lonely as a beach with nobody on it, lonely as Rapunzel shut up in a tower. There'd be no one to phone, no one to go to the beach with, no one . . .

And it might be Gran's fault. Xandra's glance at her grandmother could have scorched that lady's delicate hide, right through her pink and purple clothes.

"Your mother didn't like you having that invisible playmate," Gran was saying.

"No. She didn't. She said it was . . . "

The recollection of her mother's words stopped her short. It had been when she was standing there at the top of the stairs, listening in on her parents talking about her. She remembered her mother saying, "But Connal. It's positively spooky, that business about Flora Lee."

"Gran, why would Mom think it was spooky?"

"Don't you know? Your mother hasn't told you?"

"Told me what?" Xandra held her breath for the answer.

"Well, dear, that name was . . . "

"Was what?" Her scalp seemed to be prickling.

"Well . . . That house had belonged to a Lee family. They had a car accident where their five-year-old daughter Flora was killed."

"Their child was killed? Oh, Gran, that's so terrible." And her name was Flora. Flora Lee.

"They couldn't bear to go back to that place where they had all been so happy, so a relative handled the sale of the house for them while Mr. and Mrs. Lee were still in hospital. I believe Mr. Lee is still in and out of hospital. He was very badly hurt."

They leave you.

"So," Gran continued, "when you had that invisible playmate and called her Flora Lee, your mother thought . . . "

" . . . I was playing with a ghost?"

"No, Xandra." Gran smiled. "Your mother does not believe in ghosts; and your father was convinced that you must have heard that name from one of the neighbours and had just happened to use it for your invisible playmate."

The neighbours. The neighbour's dog. Suddenly, Xandra remembered that whenever Flora Lee appeared deep in those shadows, the neighbour's dog would go off as if he had been shot at; then he would sit down just at the edge of that little place at the foot of the garden until Flora Lee vanished.

Until the ghost left the garden?

Dogs did have a sixth sense about ghosts, didn't they? She seemed to have heard that somewhere.

So that was what it was all about — that talk downstairs when she, Xandra, had been a little kid listening in from the top of the stairs. That was why Mom had said, "Well, what she needs is a plain, ordinary, everyday visible playmate." Then the horror of it hit her. Every time they heard her talking about Flora Lee, they would have thought about that poor little girl and the Lee family. And that was why Mom had brought in Jenny.

And Flora Lee had pushed Jenny into the creek.

"I was pushed," Jenny had cried.

The way Hughie had been pushed. The way Hilary had been pushed.

NO! Flora Lee had been her made-up, invisible playmate. She, Xandra, had pushed Jenny in. Hughie and Hilary had fallen in on their own. No way was she going to start thinking she'd been playing with a ghost. Or that that ghost had anything to do with what was going on now. But . . .

"Gran, could a ghost push someone?"

"Well, a ghost is intelligent energy, so I don't see why not; though I think the push might feel more like a force."

"Like . . . a blast of air?" Hilary had said it felt more like a blast of air, hitting her right behind the knees.

Xandra had to swallow before she could ask her next question. "Gran, do you think there are ghosts?"

"Yes, I do, dear. But that doesn't mean that there are ghosts. But, there certainly are some strange happenings that are hard to explain otherwise."

"Like what?" Now that the awful subject had been brought up, she might as well hear what her grandmother had to say — not that she was prepared to go along with any of it.

"Well . . . for instance: Several months ago there was a news item in my Vancouver paper about a couple of ghosts haunting the governor's mansion in Delaware."

"A real news item? Not from one of those newspapers that say we're going to be eaten by aliens in flying saucers?"

"An item datelined 'News Service, Dover, Delaware.' I kept the clipping so you can read it yourself. Governor Castle had moved into the two-hundred-year-old governor's mansion a few months before and — "

"Recently? The haunting was recently? Not in the old superstitious days?"

"Recently. He said that the ghosts of a little girl and an old slave trader did seem to be haunting the place."

"But . . . " Xandra thought she had seen a small girl figure huddled in the corner of her own bedroom, weeping. But even if Flora Lee had been a ghost haunting her own home, she wouldn't be here, in Vancouver.

Gran was still going on with her news item: "He said that a window kept opening and the burglar alarm kept going off all night."

"Yes, but . . . " Maybe somebody who worked

there had a thing about fresh air. And a burglar alarm could malfunction, couldn't it? There was always some sensible explanation.

"At his inaugural reception there, three guests felt something tugging at their dresses. But they couldn't see anything."

Xandra felt queer in the pit of her stomach. *Something tugging at their dresses.* A little ghost could have been tugging at their dresses, trying to make someone see her. Had she seen a little ghost girl last night?

"What made it news months later, I suppose, was the fact that three sixth-graders and their teacher decided to prove, or disprove, the ghosts' existence. They moved into the mansion for one night with an array of cameras and tape recorders and a ouija board."

"Ouija board?" Xandra was not about to be convinced by something like a ouija board. "So what happened, Gran? Did they see the ghosts?"

"Well, no. They didn't see the ghosts. But their equipment didn't work. 'Their equipment went strangely awry' was the way the news service put it. And they had not been able to come up with an explanation."

"But there was an explanation," Xandra protested. "There's always an explanation. Things can happen to equipment, especially if there's someone who wants it to." She had not meant to sound shrill. But this whole thing was getting on her nerves. And there aren't any ghosts, she told herself fiercely. There's no such thing as a ghost.

But she couldn't stop herself from asking, "Gran, why would a ghost tug at the women's dresses?"

"As I understand it, the ghost wouldn't know that

she was a ghost; she wouldn't know she was invisible; she wouldn't know she didn't belong there any more. She would just be a lost, confused little spirit trying to make somebody notice her, see her, speak to her. As I understand it, a little spirit like that will cling to a familiar place or to some object she'd been fond of."

An object she'd been fond of. Could Flora Lee be clinging to the pendant? "That's mine!" she had raged when four-year-old Xandra was holding the pendant. "Put it back where you found it!" Xandra had put it back. And she should have left it there, where she found it, hidden on the rock shelf by the creek.

"Oh, oh. The pendant," she muttered, suddenly remembering that she had deliberately dropped the pendant among the potted plants. She, Xandra, DIDN'T believe in ghosts. But . . . IF Flora Lee was a real ghost clinging to the pendant, maybe she'd stay there with it. And finally get discouraged and leave. Unless, of course, she was more angry than ever about Xandra losing the pendant.

If Flora Lee was a lost, lonely, little ghost whose family had left her, she could be clinging to the pendant and to Xandra. Maybe Xandra was the only person who had ever been able to see Flora Lee and play with her. HER only friend. Maybe Flora Lee HAD pushed Jenny. Maybe she was jealous of Jenny. But . . . a ghost couldn't be jealous, could she? She couldn't be trying to get rid of people Xandra wanted to be with? To get rid of Hughie. And Hilary?

"Here's your building, dear," Gran announced. "It's been an interesting day."

Interesting? Xandra thought, angry again. Gran

would think it was "interesting," especially if she had something to do with it. But she said, "Thanks for taking me."

"Xandra, I'm always delighted to take you anywhere." Gran looked a little worried. "Would you like to come home with me?"

"Uh . . . no thanks, Gran. I want to go home and read something." Anything that would take her mind off the ghost.

So she went to the library. But the West End library didn't have a big children's section like the branches in areas where children were not classified with cockroaches. She went home and turned on the TV.

And that wasn't a great idea. She knew it was a real, black girl dancing in black leotard and tights against a black background; but nothing showed on the screen except her white gloves and white boots; so it looked like a pair of hands and a pair of feet dancing all by themselves. Really weird. She switched off the TV, made herself a peanut butter sandwich and walked over to the tennis courts. She carried her racquet, just in case.

There were some kids over there, but they all had a friend, or three friends to play with. So she went home and began reading cookbooks. Maybe she'd surprise Mom with a casserole or something.

If only the friendship with Hilary hadn't bombed.

And if only she hadn't found out that — maybe — she was haunted by a ghost.

But when she was in bed later, trying to get to sleep, Xandra thought of that lost little ghost again. A little ghost who would be more lost and confused than ever if she was clinging to that pendant over there in a flower pot on Granville Island.

That thought really bothered her. It would be dark over there now. All the shoppers would have gone home. The florists' plants would all have been put back inside. The pendant would be lying there in a big, dark, empty market where there would be nothing moving except maybe some crabs in a fish tank; and they were there waiting for someone to come along tomorrow and eat them. Everything in that enormous place was just sitting there, waiting to be eaten.

She made her mind leave the market and the pendant and the ghost girl and drift along to Sea Village, where the gleaming boats would be rocking gently beside the houseboats with their moonlit, flowering decks. She wondered what Hilary's bedroom was like.

Well, now she would never know, so she might as well forget it.

Alexandra Warwick found herself pulling the sheet over her head to smother her weeping.

Then she found herself alert for any sight or sound from that corner of the room near the dresser.

But tonight there was no huddled little figure.

Tonight, that little ghost would be huddling in a corner of the plant shop, terrified of being even more lost now than she had been before. Why didn't some bigger ghost take her away to where she should be? Why didn't somebody . . . or something . . . look after her?

Xandra sighed deeply. When she had been little, she had thought of Flora Lee as big and bossy. But Flora Lee had been only five years old, five years old and cut off so suddenly from the life she knew that she could not orient herself in the new plane — the next phase of living, or whatever Gran would call it.

Flora Lee was still only five years old. Nothing to be afraid of.

Accepting her new role of haunted heroine, Xandra sighed deeply. There was nothing to be afraid of. Then why was she shivering, in a warm bed on a warm night?

Why?

Because she knew Flora Lee was REAL. She *was* a ghost — a ghost so desperately lonely, so desperately in need of a friend that she might do anything. Especially to a girl who had deliberately dropped the treasured pendant near a busy stall where it might be trampled on . . . or anything.

Maybe she — Xandra — had better get back there tomorrow and save the pendant from kids or dogs or men with big boots or a big black raven who might carry it off and then maybe drop it into one of those cement mixers near the art school.

That's what she would do. Tomorrow. If tomorrow ever came.

To cheer up, she made herself think about that weekend at the lake with Dad. She made herself remember the way they had belted out "There was a desperado from the wild and woolly west."

But the other song floated into her mind — the snatch of song with the lovely waltz melody. And it cheered her a bit to remember Dad, there by the lake smiling as he sang, *DON'T touch my BERRIES and DON'T touch my TREES.*

Why hadn't he wanted to tell her anything about it?
Alexandra Warwick sighed deeply.
Then she cried herself to sleep.

SEVEN

"Mom, you wouldn't mind if I went over to Granville Island alone, would you?" Xandra asked next morning.

"By yourself? I would mind. Anyway I've been talking to Grandad. He wants to work with you on your tennis. And he'd like to talk to you about your school plans."

"But Mom! It's summer vacation. You don't bother about school in summer vacation."

"Xandra, by the time you're in college, you'll have to compete with kids who've been topping the lists all the way through. The dreamy kids won't stand a chance."

"So . . . I'm fated to be a loser." She was almost defiant.

"Don't use a word like that!"

"But you did, Mom. About Dad."

Xandra's mother caught her breath, swallowed and spoke in a quiet voice, "Alexandra. I was angry. When we started out, your father and I loved one another dearly. But no matter how charming someone is . . . no matter how much you love him, if he won't get down to work and carry his share of the load, a marriage — even a great marriage — disintegrates. Spend a couple of days with your grandfather, okay?"

"Okay, Mom." Actually she felt a guilty relief at not being able to rescue the pendant and the little ghost clinging to it. "I'll spend today and tomorrow with Grandad. I'll go over there as soon as I've put Hughie in day care."

"Good girl." Mom gave Xandra a quick hug before she picked up her briefcase and dashed off to crunch numbers about wood products.

It was Saturday morning before Hughie bounced his sister awake with, "Get up. Get up! We're going to Gravel Island. And I'm going on the ferry."

"We're all going on the ferry," Mom said. "Your grandmother has invited the whole family to have lunch at Isadora's, under the umbrellas."

"Oh." Going on the ferry meant that she was going to come face-to-face again with Hilary, who clearly wanted nothing more to do with Alexandra

Warwick. "Okay, Mom. What'll I wear?"

She would wear her old rose *Esprit* T-shirt and
shorts; they had been seconds from the factory outlet
because of a flaw — a sort of ghost *Esprit* below the
clear, strong name. So what if Hilary was wearing another fantastic Haida T-shirt that cost forty dollars?
She'd said she got stuff like that from her dad only because he felt guilty about leaving her and her mother.

Anyway, Hilary probably wouldn't even look at her.

At least thinking about Hilary kept her mind off
what she, Xandra, was going to do about looking for
that pendant. There wasn't much chance of that plant
being there now. In fact, maybe she was off the hook
about that whole business. So she might as well worry
about facing Hilary.

She just knew it would be THAT ferry they went
on. Gran could even have had it timed. And she
planned to be quite cool to Hilary. Oh, pleasant, of
course, but she was not going to initiate anything.
And if Hilary's father thought there was something
weird about Xandra Warwick, it wouldn't do any
harm to let him see what a nice, sensible — well, nice,
anyway — family she belonged to.

Xandra secretly looked them over as they started out
along the seawall walk. As always, Grandad was what
Mom called impeccable, slim and trim in pale shirt
and slacks; it was too hot for him to wear one of his
tweed jackets. And Mom looked great in handmade
leather sandals, geranium shirt and slacks, with those

neat abalone shell earrings that made you notice the thin green stripes in her shirt. Hughie looked scrubbed and blond in his navy blue shorts and T-shirt.

And then there was Gran.

"Do you always have to wear purple pantyhose?" Xandra asked her.

"Why not?" Gran waved it off as if there was nothing unusual about always having purple legs. Actually, in her more arty way, Gran looked almost as great as Mom did. And what was wrong with looking arty?

There were a lot of Saturday sailors out on the bay. And Grandad kept telling Hughie about the sailboats: jibs ... port tacks ... running before the wind ... "And that's the Coast Guard over there." He pointed across the narrowing bay to where a helicopter was landing on a wharf near the museums and planetarium.

"And there's the ferry," Hughie yelled as he ran toward the walkway that led to its special dock; and it was THAT ferry. There was Hilary in a baseball cap and the dangling silver earrings.

"We're going on the ferry," Hughie yelled at her as he scampered along the dock, alarming a sitting sea gull.

Hilary smiled at him. Then she leapt lightly onto the dock. "Hi," she greeted Xandra, just as if nothing had happened. But then, she was always nice to the passengers. It didn't mean a thing.

So Xandra kept her cool. "Hi," she answered quietly, standing aside to let the others in first. "Looks like a lovely day," she added, mainly to Hilary's father.

"And we're going to Izzadizzas," Hughie announced.

"Nice place," Mr. Olsen approved. He glanced very approvingly at the family, Xandra thought — especially at her mother. "Try their stuffed croissants."

"They're yummy," Hilary agreed as she started collecting the fares.

"Well," Gran said, as if that remark had just launched an idea. "why doesn't Hilary come and have stuffed croissants with us?" She looked directly at Mr. Olsen while Xandra held her breath.

"Well . . . " He was obviously ready to be persuaded. "That's very kind of you." He glanced at his daughter, eyebrows raised in question.

"I'd love to go," Hilary announced; and Xandra tried to be quiet about letting out her held breath.

"Then it's all settled," Gran said. "Meet us there at one o'clock." She took out her micro-mini-spy-glasses and began to scan the scene around her — an act that roused a vague uneasiness in her granddaughter.

The glasses had a different effect on her grandson. "Granny, did you ever be a spy?" Everybody could hear him; and when everybody looked, he beamed around at all the passengers. "Granny be'd lots of things. Granny gets hyppanized," he told anyone who was interested.

Everybody was interested. And Xandra, shrinking down into herself, noticed her grandfather's mouth. He wouldn't say anything in public, but she knew what he was thinking. And what Mom was thinking.

"Hughie. Look over there," she urged her small

brother, pointing toward some red sails.

He looked. For one second. "Granny be'd a witch once," he said as he turned back to his audience. And he didn't let up for the entire endless seven minutes. Granny had *be'd* a lady in a castle and a girl "what got put in jail for stealing bread." And that wasn't the worst of what Granny *be'd*. "But she never be'd a beaver," he assured them. It was awful. Xandra was mortified. If Hilary's Dad didn't already think that . . .

Xandra looked grimly out at the sea as they docked, too glum to appreciate the way the different blues shifted their patterns like moire silk on the surface.

"I hope Hilary is still going to have lunch with us," Gran said as they were leaving the ferry. "In spite of my lurid past."

"I'll be there," Hilary assured her with a happy grin.

With a mere nod to each of the Olsens, Xandra slipped up the ramp ahead of the others. Was Gran planning something? Something that would be bad news for a girl who desperately wanted a friend? At least Gran didn't know that Flora Lee — ghost or invisible playmate — had left the scene, along with a pendant that was probably in Timbuctoo by this time, if it wasn't crushed by a truck or ground up by one of the nearby cement mixers.

"Hey, Xandra," The hail came from up on the wharf.

Oh, no! Holbridge Herkins. There he was, beaming at her from up there. Always hanging around! And now he was waving a hand from which dangled glints of a chain. The PENDANT. Xandra felt a sudden chill along her spine.

"Xandra. Think you lost something." H.H. was positively triumphant — as if he had found her lottery ticket worth one million dollars. "You were rushing to the bus stop when you lost this."

The pendant was still around, with the ghostly little attendant spirit who was probably in a rage about the way she, Xandra, had deliberately got rid of it.

What would an enraged ghost *do*?

She stifled a groan to say, "Thanks, H.H." and take the pendant from him with a quick on/off smile as she swept right on past him. "Sorry. I'm with my family today."

"Yeh." Like he expected rejection.

In near panic at the way things were going this morning, she dropped the pendant into her shoulder bag. With its zipper broken, maybe it would fall out. And maybe no one would notice.

A brief hope. "I didn't know you had lost it, dear," Gran commented as she caught up.

"Oh . . . yeh." Xandra shrugged off such an unimportant subject, avoiding those too-observant eyes.

And thank Heaven for Hughie. "I'm going to see the boats with Grandad," he informed them, while practically jumping out of his runners with excitement, raising sea gulls and pigeons.

"This is a highly successful business area," Mom was saying. "I'd like to take a good look around."

"And I'm going with you," Xandra announced, without even a glance at their hostess.

"Good." Gran sounded delighted. "That leaves me free to do what I had in mind for this morning. Meet you at one o'clock at Isadora's."

... *What I had in mind for this morning.* Xandra switched her own mind firmly to the scene around her as she started to stroll about with her mother.

She had not realized before how many business places there were on Granville Island, nor that most of the buildings were of corrugated iron — a material that dated back to the area's days as an industrial island. But now the iron was painted blue, buff, cream, red, yellow ... And the businesses were a lot more attractive than the old grimy places must have been. Public market. Bookshops. Print workrooms. Studios, galleries and architects' offices. Theatres. Steakhouse. The Lobster Man. Yacht sales. Scuba lessons. Construction supplies filled an enormous yard with red-and-yellow cement mixers and towering yellow cranes cheek-by-jowl with the silver-grey, blue-trimmed art school.

"Nothing cutesy or touristy," Mom noted with approval. "People work here." Apparently they worked with gigantic rocks at one end of the art school; the school seemed to have grown up around the old Pier 32, right next to Sea Village. "Nice," Mom commented. "This whole place WORKS."

Which houseboat was Hilary's? Xandra wondered as they walked past Sea Village. She stifled a hopeless sigh. Maybe she would never know.

She glanced at her watch when they reached Circle Craft, a summer market for artists. Twenty to one. She was dreading one o'clock, yet she couldn't wait for it to get here. "Maybe I'll go ahead to Isadora's, Mom."

Isadora's. It even sounded like the setting for a "Big Scene." Xandra's apprehensions grew as she walked toward it. Gran was plotting something. And why did H.H. have to find that pendant and give it back to her? Today of all days?

Isadora's. Of cream-painted corrugated iron with green trim and blue-and-green umbrellas, it stood above the grassy slope of a stream. Across the plank bridge was Sutcliff Park with its balconied condominiums.

She was heading for one of the sunny benches out front when she spotted him again. "Oh, no." She couldn't have H.H. and his notebook as well as Gran and the pendant . . . and a furious little ghost.

Out there in the summer sunshine, Xandra controlled a shiver. "Please don't let anything else happen," she breathed, closing her eyes for a moment. Then opening them to see a small white dog watching her from the end of the wooden bridge.

A dog.

Why did her scalp prickle at the sight of a dog? A dog. Here . . . now . . .

EIGHT

Then she saw Hilary.

"Hi." Their guest waved just as if Xandra hadn't a grandmother who had been a witch as well as a girl "what got put in jail."

Yet it was clearly on her mind. "Has your kid brother ever got an imagination," she said as she joined Xandra on the bench. "Totally weird. But your Mom doesn't seem to be bothered about it."

"No," Xandra agreed, restraining a melodramatic sag of relief. "And your dad didn't get angry about the poltergeist and stuff?"

"Because he didn't know about it."

"You didn't tell him?"

"He doesn't believe in that kind of stuff, anyway. But I don't tell him anything that might bother his ulcer."

"Do you get ulcers from running a ferry?"

"Oh, no. His therapist suggested the ferry after he got the ulcer. Dad's into a lot of business downtown. The ferry seemed like a good idea when I was coming for the summer," Hilary went on. "Dad could never handle just sitting around doing nothing. So he signed on to run it for the owners — Oh! I see your boyfriend," Hilary added, and nodded her head toward Holbridge Herkins, now sitting near the reeds by the stream. This was a place where people could feel perfectly comfortable hanging out by themselves. But H.H. didn't make her feel comfortable.

Xandra groaned like the lady-in-distress in a school play. Then an awful thought hit her. Gran wouldn't invite him for lunch, too, would she? Him and his notebook.

"Does your grandmother really get hypnotized?" The question Xandra had been dreading.

"Well . . . yes. Anything she needs for a story. Did . . . did your dad ask about that?"

"No. I told him that she wrote kids' books. In fact, I showed him the one I bought; so he's quite impressed by your grandmother. And your grandfather looks like the admiral of the fleet or something."

Thank Heaven for sensible Grandad.

So far so good. Yet, remembering the rescued pendant, Xandra crossed her fingers. On both hands.

When she saw Gran approaching, it was like all the actors coming on stage for the final act. She felt as if her whole world was balanced on a thin pole, like one of those family acts in a circus. Maybe even an angry ghost waiting in the wings. With who knew what ghoulish trick in mind?

And then there was Gran. "Hello there," she said as she breezed by them on her way into Isadora's. "I'll make sure of the table."

For what purpose, Xandra wondered gloomily.

Xandra heard Hughie before she saw him. "Izzadizza's, Izzadizza's," he yelled, raising nearby pigeons as he ran toward the girls.

Mom came last, lugging something she had not been able to resist in Circle Craft. Grandad took the parcel from her.

"A table out back," Gran informed them when she turned up again. And was there a triumphant note in her voice? Xandra made herself breathe steadily. Nothing was going to happen. "Hughie's going to love it," Gran added as she tousled his dandelion-blow curls.

Love it? Hughie was wild with excitement about the table out back. It overlooked the water playground, a big area of paved slopes and water hoses where children were boisterously drenching one another. Those who couldn't grab one of the hoses made do with plastic buckets and yogurt cartons in several places where water was lying in small ponds.

"I hope they don't squirt us," Xandra murmured as she watched the water battles.

"I hope they do." Hughie would.

"I'm sure they would if they could reach us," his

grandmother told him. "But the umbrellas are here just to keep the sun off; and I'm sure they have another way to water the flowers." The flowers were in huge cerise-painted metal drums roped together to enclose Isadora's tables. Then, suddenly, her eyes brightened. "There's our artist." *Our* artist?

Oh, no. The woman was sitting on the grass on the other side of the water playground, wearing her khaki shirt and skirt, and sketching. She was always somewhere around when something weird happened. Xandra swallowed a rising panic.

"Maybe she's illustrating a book, with Granville Island as the setting." Gran seemed delighted.

Xandra did not. Maybe she was illustrating a children's book — Gran's book — sketching scenes Gran had set up. But that was too sinister. Even for Gran.

"This place is fun," Hilary declared, looking as if she would like to be out there with one of the water hoses.

I just hope it stays fun, Xandra thought, tensing her crossed fingers. She pushed down an eerie feeling about those water hoses. And spotting H.H. moving onto one of the benches added nothing to her peace of mind. Gran had chosen this place on purpose; and it *was* her book that the artist was illustrating, with scenes Gran had set up.

Xandra glanced again at the artist. Now looking down at her sketch pad, making quick lines. Now glancing up to look toward their table. Their table!

Don't be silly, she told herself. This was not a sinister plot. Gran wasn't a wicked witch or something — not in this life anyway. And that water could not reach them. She glanced at Mom, who was obviously bent on making this outing quality time with her children. Poor Mom.

Xandra was facing the playground, across the table from Hilary who had insisted that since she was here often, the others must have the best view seats.

Hilary quickly settled on the stuffed croissants, the kind stuffed with smoked salmon and cream cheese. Xandra settled on a different one: Miss Piggy's Ham and Cheese. And they both chose Raspberry Bang to drink. "I love the sound of the menu," Xandra giggled. But she simply could not keep her eyes off those water hoses.

The hoses were attached to what looked like genuine red fire hydrants; though what drew her gaze most often were the standing nozzles — standing metal pipes with old fashioned pump handles. You grabbed a handle, swivelled the nozzle to where you wanted it to point, and then pumped; and the water shot out in a strong stream unless you twisted the nozzle to make it come out in a short, wide spray. Two boys were playing with the standing nozzle nearest their table, alternately wrestling and spraying each other.

Gran had decided on Peter Piper's Pita Pocket. Hughie wanted Clown Face Pizza, while Mom and Grandad were closing in on Gpa: Ocean Salmon in Filo Pastry.

It was not until later, when they were eating, that Gran took out her spy glasses. Was she going to concentrate her psi powers on something? Growing apprehension had Xandra prepared to believe anything, though maybe Gran was only trying to see what those clambering nets were made of. Those nets on the hill behind the water playground had kids scrambling all over them.

H.H. was still on his bench. He still seemed to be intent on the water battles. Once, though, Xandra saw him flip through his notebook. Her stomach was full of butterflies as well as ham and cheese. She was thankful that Hilary was so busy talking to Grandad about boats that she did not need any input from a girl whose mind was whirling with poltergeists and ghosts and psychokinesis and unpredictable grandmothers.

Suddenly, the boy who had been soaked by water from the nearby nozzle grabbed the boy who had soaked him and pulled him down.

Then, at that moment, as Xandra watched, the nozzle turned. The pump handle went down. And a tremendous squirt of water reached the table, drenching Hilary's back.

Hilary! Again, Hilary!

Their equipment went strangely awry, like in Gran's newspaper clipping.

Xandra's mouth was still open as the wrestling boys jumped up. One of them grabbed the pump handle.

Hilary's mouth was open even wider than Xandra's. With shock. "Who did that?" she demanded as she jumped up. Her fists went back on her hips. "You dumb guys," she stormed. And for a moment Xandra

DAVID CAMERON ELEMENTAR
675 Meaford Avenue
Victoria, B.C.
V9B 5Y1

thought she was going to rush right out there and do something else with those fists.

"They didn't do it," Xandra blurted out. "I was watching." She caught her breath. But it was too late to take back her words.

Their equipment went strangely awry. It WAS a ghost.

Smarten up. She silently scolded herself. People often think they see what they don't really see. Like accident witnesses all "seeing" different things. She'd got herself so scared and worked up that her mind had tricked her. She'd seen what she had expected to see.

"Hilary, I am sorry. I thought that water couldn't reach this table," Mom was saying as she mopped at Hilary with the unused paper napkins.

Gran was strangely silent, strangely bright-eyed. Had SHE moved that pump handle with the power of her mind like that man on TV bending spoons with the power of his mind? Xandra flashed a furious glance at her grandmother before she followed Hilary to the washroom.

"I'm totally devastated," she moaned dramatically when they reached the paper towels. "You were our guest." Her hands moved limply, helpless in the hands of Fate. An unkind Fate.

"I'm jinxed whenever I do anything with you," Hilary answered; and her tone had the edge of a battle axe.

"But I didn't do anything," Xandra pleaded. "I wouldn't. You know I wouldn't."

Hilary almost smiled at her. "I know you didn't do it. But those boys did, and I think somebody put them up to it."

Why had she said anything? Why hadn't she just shut up and let Hilary go out there and belt those guys? "It was . . . kind of like that fish that hit you. Nobody did it. I mean . . . " Xandra faltered. "I . . . I thought I saw the nozzle turn round by itself and . . . and the pump handle go down by itself." She sagged miserably.

"You're seeing things! Those boys did it," said Hilary.

Xandra sagged even more miserably. How could you tell a girl you wanted for a friend that you were haunted by a ghost and had a grandmother who would do anything for a story? At that moment she hated Gran and her dumb research. Gran and her dumb stories.

"I know," Hilary declared with sudden fire in her eyes. "H.H.. He was out there on that bench with that notebook full of psychic craziness. I'll bet he put them up to it."

"But . . . " She couldn't let H.H. take the blame, could she? Not when she knew it was . . . Flora Lee. And Gran? "Hilary, we can't be sure it was him."

"I can. And just wait till I get my hands on that creep."

Xandra was relieved to see that H.H. was gone from the bench when they got back to the table.

"Are you all right?" Mom asked Hilary.

"I'm fine, Mrs. Warwick. But somebody else isn't going to be when I get hold of him," she said as she sat down.

"How about some peach crumble?" Gran asked. Changing the subject? Xandra wondered. "Maybe both you girls would like some?"

"Yes, please," Hilary said, obviously willing to forget the drenching. For now. "Only I think I'll sit facing the water."

Everyone laughed. Everyone except Xandra.

Hilary was so nice. She would have been a wonderful best friend, if . . . Xandra deliberately turned up the corners of her mouth. Hilary was still here.

Their equipment went strangely awry.

Flora Lee had done it. Like that little ghost at the Governor's mansion.

And Gran knew it, too.

And Hilary would have to know, before she clobbered H.H., who had probably never in his whole life done anything worse than hang around. You couldn't let him take the blame for what . . . what an angry ghost girl had done. Gran and the ghost, together, ruining her life.

"Are you going to kill that guy?" Hughie asked Hilary.

"Nope. But I'm going to kill somebody if things don't stop happening to me."

Xandra could see Mom wondering *what things?*

"Uh . . . Hilary," she butted in before her friend could start talking about getting hit with a fish that nobody threw and getting pushed into the sea by a blast of air right behind her knees. Mom might think Hilary was not a suitable friend. "Uh . . . Granville Island must be the most wonderful place to live . . . especially on a houseboat," she blustered on just to say something, anything not about weird stuff.

"When I'm not being a target, it's great," Hilary declared. And — thank Heaven — she began chatting about life on Granville Island. She'd even taken a couple of sailing lessons, she told them.

Hilary looked at her watch. "Oh, oh. I have to get home. We're going out on the *Kanu*. Dad wants to leave before three and I have to pack my sea bag. Thanks for the lunch," she said to Gran. "Bye," she said, as she skirted the water playground.

With Xandra close behind her. "I'll walk to the houseboat with her," she called back to her mother. "You're nearly dry," she assured Hilary. Then trying not to sound as anxious as she felt, she ventured to ask, "Are you going to tell your father about getting drenched?"

"Are you kidding? No way." Hilary knew how to handle an ulcer. "We're heading for the Gulf Islands this afternoon. Coming back Monday night. So I'll have to wait until Tuesday to settle the score with H.H. Do you want to come over on Tuesday afternoon?"

To help settle the score with H.H? An instant's alarm could not stem Xandra's wild burst of joy at the invitation. "Yes. I'd like to," she assured Hilary.

Things were looking better.

"I'm sure Mom will let me come over by myself," Xandra added, trying to sound as certain as Hilary would have sounded.

"Great. See you on Tuesday." Hilary made it official. "And right now I'd better run. Dad'll want to hoist sail out beyond the bridge at three o'clock."

"Okay. I'll come with you." She was dying to know which houseboat was Hilary's. Which houseboat she, Alexandra Warwick, was actually going to visit.

"That's ours," Hilary pointed out when they reached Sea Village. It was in the outer row, farther

out into False Creek — a handsome brown house with
geraniums blazing on the end of the sun deck Xandra
could see from the wharf. There was a sleek white
sailboat moored alongside. The *Kanu.*

"Wow," Xandra breathed.

"I'll show you over it on Tuesday," Hilary promised. "Right now I have to pack. Okay?"

Tuesday. She was coming to visit on Tuesday. She
had a friend. So she wasn't going to be lonely again
all summer. Maybe she and Hilary wouldn't be together all the time; but when you had a best friend,
you didn't feel lonely even when you couldn't be with
her. You had things to think about, things to phone
about. Xandra could have done a handstand right
there on the wharf.

Until she remembered *just wait till I get my hands
on H.H.* She simply could not let him take the blame
for what a ghost had done. But . . . but if she told Hilary that it was a ghost that had soaked her — and
pushed her, and hit her with a fish — Hilary would
think she was crazy. It would be the end of the friendship. Before it had really begun.

What was she going to do?

"See you," Hilary called as she started down the
ramp.

"See you." In spite of having enough troubles to
sink a barge, Xandra called out her answer. "What
time shall I come?"

"Catch the twelve o'clock run and we'll have
lunch out on deck."

Lunch on the deck with her BEST FRIEND.

Heading back to Isadora's, she tried to stop thinking

about Hilary's coming reaction to what she, Xandra, would have to tell her to get H.H. off the hook. By the time she reached the restaurant, she was sagging like a wet flag on a rainy day.

WHAT was she going to do?

NINE

"Hilary's a charming girl," Mom commented, after she and Xandra had said good-night to Hughie.

"She's great." Xandra paused. "Mom, you can see why I always want to go over to Granville Island," she continued, embroidering facts only a little. "Hilary and I roam around having fun while Gran makes her notes. And Mom! Hilary has invited me to have lunch out on her sun deck on Tuesday. I said I could go. And I don't need to have Gran take me. I don't, Mom."

"Of course, you don't, dear, as long as Hilary will

promise to meet you right at the wharf."

"And Mom, can we just keep this to ourselves? I don't want anybody making plans to go over there Tuesday."

"Not a word," Mom willingly promised. "What time will you be back?"

"I'll have to let you know when I get there. They're off cruising the Gulf Islands right now."

"Okay. As long as I have the address and phone number."

"No problem."

No problem?

No. No problem apart from having to get through the next three nights.

During each of those nights, Xandra woke up suddenly, sure that she had heard weeping. But, each time, there was no weeping . . . no one huddled in the corner of the room. It was just her imagination.

Then there was the pendant.

Xandra did not want to carry it around with her, in a pocket or in her shoulder bag. And she certainly did not want to put it into her treasure chest with all those other keepsakes.

Yet . . . she didn't really want to leave it on top of the chest of drawers, where she would keep seeing it.

So she did all three things in turn.

And when Tuesday arrived and it was time to head for the ferry, she made up her mind. If Hilary was still threatening a bad end for H.H., she, Xandra, might need the pendant. Maybe Flora Lee would do something to Hilary and Hilary would have to believe her. She dropped the pendant into her shoulder bag. And before she had walked three blocks, Xandra wished she had left it at home.

Flora Lee might do something terrible to Hilary. She wished she had the guts to hurl it into the sea like the poor fisherman's copper urn with the genie in it. And just in case she might, and then live to regret it, Xandra sprinted along the dock to where the noon ferry was coming in.

Hilary was waiting on the dock at Granville Island.

"Your dad's missing a great sailing breeze," the ferryman told Hilary as she reached forward to steady the boat. "Looks like it might blow up later, though," he added as he scanned the sky.

"Dad's downtown," Hilary explained to her guest with a conspiratorial air. "So we're totally on our own."

Totally on their own? Holbridge Herkins was hovering up there on the wharf with his notebook. Oh dear. Now Hilary would want to settle scores with him. Poor guy. When he hadn't done anything except be a pest.

"We'll ditch him for now," Hilary confided. She really didn't seem to hold grudges like some girls. "We'll go out in the boat after lunch."

Xandra caught her breath. "Not in the sailboat?" They couldn't be going out, by themselves.

"No. I have my own dinghy."

Her dinghy was a rowboat tied up near the sailboat, its oars secured along the bottom and a light outboard motor mounted on its stern. "Dad lets me puddle around in it whenever I like since I have my bronze badge in swimming. As long as I wear my life jacket. Anyway, can you swim?"

"Of course." Xandra could swim very well. In a pool. And today she was a free spirit, wasn't she? She was going to act as free and breezy as Hilary. And as CONFIDENT. Today she would throw herself into the adventurer role and play it with gusto. Hilary wouldn't want a squeaky mouse as a friend. "That would be fun!" Xandra the actor was jubilant.

"Let's go inside," Hilary said, as they reached the houseboat.

It was an elegant house, with dark leather couches on a brilliant sunburst rug under a skylight.

"You fix up the chairs and table on the deck so H.H. can't see us if he comes around and I'll get the sandwiches. Fresh crab and hard-boiled egg. And I hope you like lemonade."

"I love it," Xandra assured her hostess. She loved everything: the houseboat, the boats going by, lunch out on the deck, quiet music from the radio and — most of all — the prospect of a whole afternoon with just the two of them together.

She was so intent on enjoying things and on getting into a suitably adventurous spirit by watching kayakers paddling by in False Creek that she scarcely noticed when a marine bulletin broke into the music on the radio. In any case, "small craft warning" didn't mean a thing to landlubber Xandra; craft was pottery and weaving in her world.

Things were going to be wonderful. At long, long last, things were going to be wonderful.

She had noticed that the sky was not as cloudless as it had been. But you couldn't have everything. Today was a perfect day. And though Mom had insisted she take along a sweater, she was more than warm enough in just her T-shirt and shorts.

"Have you ever rowed?" Hilary asked as she came out with the lunch tray.

"No. But Grandad has promised to teach me."

"Maybe I'll beat him to it."

"Great." False Creek was not very wide. You'd never be far from shore out there; and Xandra could do eight laps like nothing.

The sandwiches were as luscious as they were expected to be, especially when you were eating them out on deck with geraniums and nasturtiums all around you, and boats . . . "I'd love to live on a houseboat," she said, controlling an envious sigh.

"Next time bring your p.j.'s."

Next time. Xandra joyously sipped her lemonade from a glass with an anchor on it. Next time. Her lonely days were over. "You have a motor on the dinghy," she noted, by way of keeping her cool.

"Yeh. One cylinder," Hilary wrinkled her nose. "That's why I call her *The Tortoise*. Can't race anything faster than a lame duck."

That was fine with Xandra. She didn't want to race anything faster than a lame duck.

Hilary licked a finger and held it up. "Wind's from the northwest," she announced.

"Is that good?"

"Doesn't matter much when you haven't got sail on." Hilary was so nautical, though she had said that this was her first summer with boats, hadn't she? "Wish I had a sail on the dinghy."

Xandra waved off the lack of a sail. "I think it's great to go rowing." Or even motoring, as long as it was a motor with only one cylinder.

"Dad lets me sail a bit when we're out in the *Kanu*. Is it ever fun. Maybe we could take you along on our next cruise."

"Great." Things were really looking up for Alexandra Warwick.

It was after two when they put on their life jackets and got into the dinghy. Xandra stowed her shoulder bag under the seat. Hilary pushed off and started getting the oars into the oarlocks, ready to row. As soon as they had nosed out of their mooring, Xandra could see H.H. sitting up there on one of the wharf benches, just watching. Maybe he needed a friend, too.

"Sorry, H.H.," Hilary giggled, with a nod in his direction. "You can't tell us about psychokinesis today." She looked at Xandra. "You don't believe in all that stuff, do you?" she asked point blank.

"Well . . . I've read about people who can move things by the power of their minds. I read about a girl in South America who could lift rocks by just looking at them. And in yesterday's paper there was a piece about a fourteen-year-old girl in Ohio who kept getting hit by flying objects like clocks and candlesticks; and even when an electrician taped down electrical switches in her house, lights kept turning on and radios and TVs suddenly blasting out. All by themselves. I guess some of that could be true."

"Weird." Hilary didn't seem to mind weird so much

when it was away off in South America or Ohio.

"As long as you don't get hit with a flying flower pot or something," Xandra went on, trying to laugh the whole thing off.

"I'm going to make sure I don't get hit with anything," Hilary informed her guest. "We're going out under the bridge." She nodded toward the spot where the boats motored out into English Bay. "H.H. won't even be able to see us out there, much less work his psychokinesis hocus-pocus."

It was her — Xandra's — fault that Hilary thought it was H.H. she had to get away from if she didn't want to get hit again. Xandra looked out into the Bay. "Does your Dad let you go out there?"

"Well. You know how parents are. But he's not here to have his ulcer stirred up."

"Right." Xandra agreed with all the robust spirit a squeaky mouse could summon up for an adventurer role. Give it all you've got she reminded herself.

As soon as they were well clear of the floats and were out in the creek, Hilary stowed the oars in the bottom of the dinghy. Kneeling down, she pulled the cord to start the motor. It sputtered into action, then died. "Sometimes it does this at the first pull," she told Xandra. And pulled again. This time it went. "You sit up forward."

As Xandra stood up to move to the seat in the bow, she rocked the boat.

"Don't stand!" Hilary ordered. "Keep low. Grasp the gunnel and crawl."

Xandra was more than willing to crawl, and to grasp the sides of the boat as she crawled. She had not realized how tippy a small boat was.

Hilary settled down in the stern and took the tiller like an old salt. "English Bay, here we come." She had the look of a Haida adventurer as she headed for the bridge. Utterly confident.

"Here we come!" Xandra echoed with fake enthusiasm.

"Sort of muggy here in the Creek," Hilary remarked. It was why they had left their sweaters in the houseboat. "But wait until we get into the bay."

Xandra could wait. But there wasn't much else she could do about it, now that she had gone along with letting H.H. be the one they had to get away from. Guilt over that deception made her uneasy; something bad might come as punishment.

They *br-r-r-r-red* along past wharf restaurants with their umbrellas, past the market . . .

A big sailboat slipped by them with sails furled.

"You aren't allowed to do more than five knots in The Creek," Hilary informed her. "But don't worry. We couldn't do five knots if we were trying to get away from a sea monster."

That was fine with Hilary's crew, who concentrated on some pennants whipping out from masts in the public marina, because that helped her with her adventurer spirit. And as they went under the bridge, she could hear the traffic rumbling by overhead.

"There's the Coast Guard, to port," Hilary said as she pointed to its rescue cutters tied to a wharf on their left. The station's flag was whipping out briskly.

But in the shelter of False Creek and then in the lea of the shore, the girls felt nothing more than little gusts of wind. They could not yet see the immensity of English Bay. And Xandra, the total landlubber, thought nothing of the few white patches of foam out there where she could see.

"This is something like it," Hilary sang out. Her eyes were sparkling.

"Right," Xandra managed to echo her friend's enthusiasm as she hunched in the bow. She had never before realized how big the bay was. You'd need to do a lot more than eight laps there if you fell in.

"We'll head for that freighter out there."

It did not look far, but Grandad had said that it was hard to judge distance on the water.

Xandra looked at the freighters that were always anchored out in the bay, waiting for their turn to load at the docks in the city's inner harbour. But it was the sailboats that caught her attention. They looked as if they were going to topple right over any minute. She mentioned them to Hilary.

"It's fun when you're heeled over like that," was her friend's reaction. "As long as you're not trying to slurp hot soup." She was so free, so unafraid of anything.

"Uh . . . how long will it take us to reach that freighter?" Xandra asked with all the bright interest she could muster. It looked just as far away.

"With this motor, who knows?"

For the next few minutes they did not talk much. Those little waves were getting bigger. The dinghy's pitching was getting steeper, too — nosing up, then slapping down. Yet Hilary seemed unconcerned as she headed straight into the waves, making for the freighter. The bridge began to look awfully far back to a girl who could do eight laps like nothing. When

there were no waves. Xandra began to wish she had
worn her sweater. She hid her hand as she crossed
her fingers.

Then promptly uncrossed them. Hadn't crossing
your fingers come from the time when people had
made it a sign of the cross to ward off evil spirits? Very
deliberately she licked her lips and started belting out a
sea song she and Dad had had fun with at that cabin:

"A rollicking ship for an ocean trip
Was the walloping Window Blind."

If you kept your shoulders jigging in time with the
song, she noticed, they did not get so hunched up.

Hilary grinned at her and joined in when she got
to the chorus:

"So blow ye wind hi ho!
A-roving we will go.
We'll stay no more on GRANVILLE'S shore.
So let the music play-ay-ay!"

"Wow!" Xandra gasped when the big seas hit
them. The bow went up sharply. And it slapped down
only to be hit by the breaking of the next wave as
they nosed into it. Spray came into the boat, drenching Xandra. And now she realized what those white
patches of foam had been — the breaking crests of
waves. She'd have crossed all her fingers if they had
not been hanging on so fiercely to the gunwale.

Then, without conscious thought, she did let go.
Bracing herself, she quickly reached under her seat
for her shoulder bag. She looped the strap of her bag
under her belt and tied it securely. Then she grabbed
the sides of the boat again.

"You look like a wet hen," Hilary joked.

"So what's a hen doing at sea?" Xandra managed to joke back. What really worried her were the sounds of the motor. As the dinghy nosed down into a trough and the stern came up, lifting the propeller out of the water, the little motor roared alarmingly; then it sputtered. Yet Hilary showed no sign of turning back. She just kept them pitching on and on and on toward the freighter.

Every so often they hit another breaking wave, drenching her.

Then they hit a really big one. And this time, when the stern came up, lifting the propeller out of the water, the motor roared. Spluttered. DIED.

Hilary's bravado — if it had been bravado — left her. Yet she did not panic. She immediately grabbed the starting cord. Pulled it. And nothing happened.

Now Xandra was not only a wet hen; she was a petrified wet hen, huddled down in the bow, grasping the gunwale, her attention all on Hilary.

Hilary pulled the cord again. Nothing. "Out of gas," she gasped; and for the first time, she sounded alarmed. "I forgot to check. Dad'll kill me."

"As long as he gets the chance to kill you," Xandra managed to joke.

With no motor to push the dinghy forward, it turned sideways; and now, broadside on to the sea, it was knocked and blown about like a toy boat. When a breaking wave hit it, it pitched violently on its side, almost capsizing. Xandra grabbed for the high side and hung on for dear life, watching Hilary.

Thrown from side to side, Hilary was on her knees, frantically scrambling to get the oars out.

Then the squall hit. The wind almost took their
breath away as it caught the spray and flung it back
into their faces.

Somehow, Hilary managed to get the oars out,
then into their open rollocks. She had to get the boat
head-on to the seas again to keep it from being capsized. A job for a strong and experienced oarsman,
Xandra suspected, not for a girl — however valiant —
in her first summer with boats.

In Hilary's attempt at the first pull, one oar
missed the water. And the force of her pull threw her
back and the end of the oar whacked her in the
chest. She struck the side of her head on the gunwale
and lay still in the bottom of the boat.

Xandra, equally stunned without the whack on the
head, watched helplessly as the oars slid out into the
water.

TEN

Panic gripped Xandra.

No oars.

No motor.

Hilary knocked out.

But just for a moment.

"Hilary! Are you okay?" Gasping her relief as her friend stirred, Xandra scrambled to help her. Was hurled down on top of her. And with the weight all on one side, the dinghy was thrown onto its beam ends. The force of the wind struck the exposed bottom. Capsized the boat. Dumped the girls into the sea. Into the shock of the deep, cold water. The shock of the wild, cold spray.

Buoyed by its floatation, the dinghy's ridge of keel and its forward hull stayed above water.

Gasping in the shock of the wild sea, the girls were almost touching the capsized boat. Xandra, panicked by the cold, was spluttering to catch her breath in the wind and the spray. She made a grab for the boat; but there was nothing to grab on its slick surface. And the surge of the sea swept her away from it.

"Hilary! Hilary!" she screamed.

Hilary, who had been closer to the stern, had grasped the sunken propeller shaft. Xandra had one glimpse of her face. Groggy!

Swept away from the boat and accustomed to nothing rougher than a swimming pool, she was terrified by the violence of the wind, the violence of the water, and by the thought of the depth of the water beneath her. The cold, dark, depths of the water down there. Frantically she tried to swim back to the boat.

Constantly thrown up and down by the unrelenting violence, gasping and choking as water dashed into her mouth, she was swept farther and farther away; while the dinghy seemed to stay almost where it was, just rising and sinking with Hilary hanging on.

She had to get back to it. But she couldn't get back to it. She flailed her arms and kicked her legs, and she just kept getting farther and farther away from the dinghy, farther and farther away from Hilary.

Half the time Xandra couldn't catch her breath. And with her hair constantly whipped across her face, half the time she couldn't see. She kept losing sight of the dinghy. It was there. Then it wasn't there. She didn't know where it was. And she was cold. Cold as a corpse. Cold as a corpse.

But she must not panic. Alone in the fierce, unrelenting sea, she must not panic. She must get back to the dinghy. Get back to Hilary.

But she couldn't see the boat. And she was so cold!

She couldn't see the dinghy, and she didn't know where to swim. But she had to keep moving. SHE HAD TO FIND HILARY!

If only she didn't keep gulping the water flung into her face!

If only she could see Hilary! Maybe Hilary was drowned. But you couldn't drown with a life jacket on . . . Could you?

She tried to swim, but her arms were now too heavy to lift. She had to keep her head up, to see the dinghy, to see Hilary.

She couldn't breathe! She was going to suffocate. She was going to die out here, alone in the fierce, cold water because she couldn't breathe.

The world seemed to be darkening around her. And she couldn't breathe. She was drifting off somewhere . . . drifting like vapour . . . bright swirling vapour drifting upward into a golden brightness . . . and it was lovely to drift into the golden brightness.

Suddenly she sensed someone touching her . . . someone stopping her drift upward into the golden brightness . . . someone holding her steady in the wild sea. And with the calm vagueness of a dream, she looked back over her shoulder.

A girl. A little girl who seemed vaguely familiar. A little girl with red hair. And as a strange calm seemed to flood through her, Xandra gave herself up to the dream of drifting with the girl . . . drifting through the bright swirling vapour with wild roses and forget-me-nots and violets and bluebells all swirling mistily together with green vines . . .

Then, in the dream, she heard a faint roar that grew louder and louder, like a motorboat coming toward her in the dream.

Then she sensed hands pulling her out of the vapour . . . out of the cold dark sea. Strong hands . . . strong arms were lifting her out of the sea.

She blinked, as though waking from a dream. Men. Uniformed men. Slowly her mind focused. The Coast Guard. She was on a Coast Guard cutter . . . Now swathed in a blanket, she was being carried down into a cabin. A warm cabin. She was laid on a bunk.

"There's another girl," she breathed to the man who was tucking blankets around her.

"We've got her," he answered; and Xandra saw Hilary over on the other bunk in the cabin. "She reached you just before we did."

Vaguely she knew that Hilary was talking to her, "Xandra! Are you all right?"

But her mind was on . . . "Another girl," she told the man. "She — " The roar of the engine stopped Xandra. And a sudden realization. *That other girl had been little . . . and she had been untouched by the sea's vio-*

lence; her red hair had been dry and still in the fierce wind.

"Come on, now." They were urging her to sip the tea, the hot, sweet tea. "Just a little sip."

"Is she all right?" Hilary's voice again. Anxious. "And what about the dinghy?"

"We've got your boat out on the well deck," a man's voice answered.

Xandra was conscious of someone talking to Hilary. And Hilary's answers: No. There had been no one else with them. No. There were no parents at home to phone to. And the engine was roaring on and on. Then there was another sound. The far-off scream of a siren... off somewhere... a siren. Xandra huddled down deeper into her warm blankets.

She tried to answer their questions, tried to talk to Hilary. But that other girl filled her thoughts. A little girl with red hair. Smiling at her. Unbuffetted by the fierce sea.

Flora Lee? Did Flora Lee have red hair?

The engine stopped. Other men came aboard. And as she was lifted onto a stretcher, Xandra heard Hilary, in command again, protesting that she could walk out. "I'm totally O.K."

"That's great, but why walk when you can ride?" a man's voice coaxed. And Hilary was carried out. Still protesting.

Xandra glimpsed H.H. up on the wharf. "Him!" Hilary cried out. "It was him!"

"It sure was him," a pleasant voice assured her. "That kid nearly knocked himself out getting over here to give the alarm." He had seen the girls go out under the bridge; and then, when he'd caught a small craft warning on a radio, he had run over from Granville Island, all the way around the marina and the railway tracks. "That's quite a friend you've got there," the voice finished admiringly.

Xandra gave H.H. a wan smile as she was carried past him. She would have to tell Hilary that — what would she tell Hilary? Hilary would think she was crazy. But she would have to say something; she simply could not let him take the blame for this accident or for the ones that had come before it.

Then they were in the ambulance, screaming their way to the hospital.

"I don't need a hospital," Hilary kept insisting. But with no parent at home, she had no choice in the matter. She was going to the hospital.

Xandra's mother came to the hospital as soon as she got the phone call. "Darling," she breathed, holding her daughter close. And Xandra found herself dissolving into tears. That was all she wanted now. Just to be held tightly, and then taken home to her own bed.

The next day, when Gran was keeping an eye on her, Xandra faced the haunting memory of *that other girl*. That was FLORA LEE who had been out there in the wild sea. I did see her! I did!

Yet . . .

She reached you just before we did. Hilary had

reached her just before the Coast Guard got there. Had it been Hilary she'd seen out there? She wanted to talk about Flora Lee with her grandmother. And she wanted some answers from her grandmother. Was Gran part of it?

She broached the subject hesitantly. "Gran . . . a lot of weird things have been happening lately."

"Yes, indeed." To Gran, weird was fascinating.

But her granddaughter found the current weirdness about as fun-filled as a dumped dinghy. Her anger flared. "Gran. What were you researching over there on Granville Island?"

Her grandmother looked at her for a moment. "Yes. Well, it changed as I went along, dear. I started out with the idea of the return of old native trickster spirits that had been displaced from the local forests and streams when the trees were cut down."

"Trickster spirits? You mean . . . you thought trickster spirits were doing all that pushing and stuff?"

"Oh no. Nobody had been pushing anybody when I started working on the idea. It was only after those strange things began happening to you and Hilary that I decided to do a little detecting."

"But what was happening? Why was it happening? Who was doing it?" Xandra asked shrilly, the words tumbling out.

"I don't know for sure, Xandra. For a while there, I suspected that artist who always seemed to be hanging around you girls, supposedly just doing action sketches.

"But you don't suspect her now?"

"Well, she wasn't around when Hughie said he was pushed in. And seemed as surprised as I was when Hilary was pushed. And I was watching her when Hilary was hit with the fish. She looked as shocked as I felt."

"I just know H.H. didn't do those things," Xandra was determined to exonerate him. "He didn't push Hilary in and he didn't squirt that hose."

Her grandmother had said she was shocked. But was she really? Maybe she COULD move objects with the power of her mind and those spy glasses. Maybe she could bring a GHOST in on cue!

"What is it, Xandra?"

"Gran, did you do any of those things . . . you know . . . trying out something to see if it would work for your story?"

Her grandmother gave her a quick hug. "No, dear. But I can see why you would suspect me. I knew you wanted Hilary to be your friend — that's why I invited her to have lunch at Isadora's with us. But I was as puzzled by it all as you were. At first."

"At first? So if you weren't doing those weird things, who was?"

Before she could answer the question, Gran sniffed toward the kitchen. "Something's burning." She dashed off.

"So what else is new?" Xandra merely mouthed the words. Gran was always burning cakes or cookies or whatever. Xandra knew the answer anyway. With every living suspect crossed off the list, the identity of the real culprit was certain. A lost, angry little ghost girl.

She lay back on the cushions. As it so often did, her mind turned toward thoughts of her father.

Gran came out of the kitchen. She crossed the

living room and opened the balcony door to let the smoke out. She glanced twice at her watch.

"Gran, do you know where Dad is right now?"

"No. I don't. But I do know that he's got a surprise for you, soon."

"Oh, Gran! Tell me."

"Dear, it's not my secret to tell."

Xandra's imagination had switched instantly to her worry mode. "Is something wrong with Dad?"

"No, Xandra, nothing's wrong with your dad."

But . . . his letters were infrequent, loving, amusing with funny little bits about van travel, yet never saying anything about his dreams . . . or her dreams. Maybe Mom had made him promise not to keep his daughter's head "in the clouds" with foolish ideas. That was it. He had promised Mom. After all, she was supporting the children; and she wouldn't have to tell Dad that twice. Oh dear. WHY did things have to change?

At that moment, the pale, sun-screening curtains billowed in from the glass doors to the balcony.

Xandra caught her breath. The back of her neck prickled.

She knew there was no sound from those billowing curtains. Yet she also knew that an angry little voice said, "You LEFT me. For that girl! And you lost my pendant!"

The curtains billowed outward this time, outward to the balcony. Then they hung as still as curtains painted on a stage set. An angry little ghost had gone through.

The pendant! Xandra remembered looping the strap of her shoulder bag around her belt. It must have come off when she was in the water. The pendant was in the bag and the bag was somewhere at the bottom of English Bay. This time, it was really lost and the haunted one stifled a groan as she lay back against the cushions. Too weak to think about a lost pendant.

Too weak to think about what she was going to tell Hilary?

How she wished that someone else would give her the lines to say. But in real life, nobody ever did give you your lines. YOU had to figure out what to say. And then throw yourself into English Bay.

Without a life jacket.

AFTER she had told Hilary what she had to tell her and lost hope forever of having her for a best friend.

ELEVEN

If she was going to get H.H. off the hook without scaring Hilary off with news about a ghost, Xandra was going to have to really think this thing through. Hilary wouldn't believe anybody could make things fly through the air. Or why she should be the target. She, Xandra, was going to have to think and think and think. But not right now.

"Xandra," Gran said as she sat down on the sofa beside her. "I want to tell you something. The real estate agent who sold your house called your mother yesterday." She paused, then went on. "She knows the Lees, and thought that your mother would like to know that Mr. Lee had died."

"Oh, Gran! That's terrible."

The intercom buzzed. Gran answered the summons. "It's Hilary," she said. "I'm going out to get some groceries while she's here. You'll be all right?"

"Sure, Gran."

Hilary walked in, carrying a bunch of flowers from Granville Island. And looking, for once, a little hesitant. "Xandra, are you okay now? I'm sorry. You could have drowned, and it was all my fault. I did everything wrong." She added ruefully, "And I think I gave Dad another ulcer."

She reached you just before we did, the Coast Guard man had said.

"But you saved my life, Hilary," Xandra said, a trifle wanly, as befitted one who had nearly vanished into the swirling vapours.

"The Coast Guard saved your life. I just got to you when they found us. I should have stayed with the boat, but I just had to try to find you."

"Hilary, it was not all your fault," Xandra answered. "It's probably all my fault." She had not really wanted to say that. Not before she had figured this thing out.

"Your fault?" Hilary looked astonished. "How do you figure that?"

"Well," Xandra said, not very happily, "you thought it was H.H. you had to get away from if you didn't want to get drenched or pushed or something." Xandra's mind grabbed wildly about for a next line. Something. Anything.

"And it wasn't him?" A police investigator could not have looked at her more uncompromisingly. Hilary was getting back to her old self. Fast.

"No. It wasn't H.H. who was making those weird things happen." she sagged miserably. What was she going to say next? "No. It wasn't H.H. . . . "

"Then who was it?" The questioner narrowed her eyes, ready for whoever had caused those accidents.

"It was . . . " What on earth could she say? She simply could not tell Hilary that she was sure it was a ghost. Hilary would walk out in nothing flat. "It's . . . it's hard to tell you because . . . because you don't like things that don't have an ordinary explanation." Telling Hilary would have been easier if she, Xandra, were a dying heroine or something. But she wasn't a dying heroine.

"Well," Hilary defended herself. "I don't like being pushed into the water, and I don't like being hit in the ear with a fish. And I don't like not knowing who did it! But, . . . I was scared every time I walked out on you that you wouldn't want me back as a friend."

"Scared? You? You've never been scared in your life." Astonishment raised Xandra's protest a couple of octaves. "I thought you wouldn't want me back as a friend because of all the awful things that happened to you when I was around."

"Look. I don't believe in ghosts and poltergeists and stuff . . . but H.H. is pretty weird. Maybe he figured out how to do some of those things. I don't know! . . . But what are you trying to say?" Her direct, steady gaze demanded an answer.

Xandra did not yet have an answer ready. But with those steady blue eyes on her, she had to say something. "Well . . . " She took a deep breath.

And she was saved by the bell. The telephone. It was Mom, just checking up on her. When she heard that Hilary was there, she wanted to ask her how she was; and then Hilary wanted to apologize for endangering Xandra. She was just hanging up when Gran walked in.

"I'll have to talk to you later," Xandra whispered to Hilary, weak with relief at the reprieve. She still did not know what she dared to say about the ghost.

The intercom buzzed.

"That'll be Dad," said Hilary. "He was just giving me time to see how you are and — Hi, Dad. I'll be right down — and to tell you that I've got a surprise when you're well enough to come over." She glanced inquiringly at Gran.

"I think she'll be in good shape by tomorrow."

"Great!" Hilary sang out. "It's something we're going to do," she added with a conspiratorial wink at Gran. "Just a little adventure." She waved good-bye as she rushed out the door.

If that "little adventure" was going to be anything like the one in *The Tortoise*, Xandra hoped she'd never be in good shape. But Hilary was just the kind to say that if you had been scared at sea, then you ought to get right back out there on the sea again. Like getting back up on a horse after you had been bucked off. And Xandra would have to pretend that . . .

Why would she have to pretend? Maybe that was her whole trouble. She spent her life pretending. Always an actor in a play. It was great to pretend when you were up there on the stage. But maybe it wasn't so great to spend your whole life acting.

So what was she going to tell Hilary?

The intercom startled her into action. "Oh hi, H.H.. Come on up." She buzzed him in.

And was surprised to see him clutching a bunch of daisies instead of a notebook. And three cardboard tubes.

"You're quite a hero, Holbrook," Gran greeted him, "racing around to alert the Coast Guard. Sit down. Would you like some milk and cookies?"

Cookies. So that was what the burnt smell had been. But a plateful of burnt cookies did not phase Gran in the slightest. So the cookies were chocolate chip and charcoal. So what else was new? H.H. took one while Gran busied herself putting the flowers into a blue vase near Hilary's flowers.

Only nibbling at the cookie, he seemed a bit fidgety about something. Obviously delaying something awful he had to say, he handed her one of the cardboard tubes. "That artist asked me to give these to you and Hilary."

She twisted whatever it was out of the tube. "A sketch of me! Look, Gran."

"It's charming. That was kind of her. Did she do one of you, too, Holbrook?"

"Yeh." With obvious reluctance, H.H. twisted the sketch of himself out of the tube. Then, looking about as happy as a bug stuck on a pin, he unrolled it. "With my nose stuck in my notebook. As usual. No wonder you and Hilary didn't want to talk to me."

Xandra felt the warmth of a guilty flush spreading over her neck and face.

"Xandra," he rushed on. "I guess I'm the disturbed adolescent making all those weird things happen to Hilary," he said, gloomy as a haunted house. "I . . . well, I guess it was a poltergeist and — "

Knowing what he was going to say and desperate to make him feel better about himself, Xandra broke in with, "No. It wasn't exactly a poltergeist. It was something to do with me."

"Not you," he protested. "You're too nice to want to hurl a fish or push people or . . . all that stuff. It was ME," H.H. said. "Me wanting to get rid of Hilary so you'd talk to me."

Xandra opened her mouth to protest. But Gran said it for her. "Nonsense. You're not disturbed. You're just lonely."

"Well, I . . . you know . . . I am kind of short on friends." He stopped. Then he said firmly, "Nope. . . . I'm the disturbed adolescent."

Hilary would believe that in a flash.

But — poor guy. Xandra found herself saying, "You're not disturbed. Nobody is," she went on miserably, "because a ghost did it."

"A ghost? But . . . " Incredulity seemed to be battling with relief. "A ghost on Granville Island?"

Xandra took a deep breath and plunged in. "Look, I've got something to tell you . . . you and Hilary. But not 'til tomorrow. Okay?" She leaned wanly back against the cushions.

H.H. got the hint. "Yeh. Okay," he agreed.

"I'm going over to see Hilary tomorrow morning.

If you'll just sort of hang around over there, I'll find a chance to tell you both what I have to tell you."

"Okay. I'll be there tomorrow." He was still blinking his puzzlement as he closed the door.

Tomorrow she was going to get this all sorted out.

Yeh. Sorted out for a long, lonely summer. No way Hilary would want a friend who thought she had a ghost hovering near her — particularly a ghost who seemed bent on getting rid of Ms. Hilary Olsen.

At least she would be getting H.H. off the hook. H.H. was a guy with enough troubles without thinking he was a poltergeist's energizer.

"Gran, that pendant. It was Flora Lee's," Xandra blurted out. "You knew that, didn't you? But, Gran, it was in my shoulder bag and I must have lost it in English Bay. Her pendant. The thing she was clinging to. Poor little girl!"

"Yes. But there's nothing you can do about the pendant. Maybe she'll leave it and move on, now that it's not in a familiar place, or with a familiar person. And Xandra, her father has died, too. No doubt he'll search for his little daughter. We should feel happy about that."

Xandra felt very happy, once she had time to think about it. If the ghost was gone, or about to go, why did she need to risk her friendship with Hilary by telling her about it? She could just say to Hilary and H.H. that her mind was wandering because of the accident. They'd probably believe her, she thought ruefully.

"She could always come back," Gran was saying.

"What!"

"I mean in a future lifetime."

"Oh. That." As long as it wasn't this summer. Then.

The gossamer curtains billowed in so suddenly that she caught her breath. But — Flora Lee was gone, wasn't she? Gone with her beloved pendant. So why did she sense anger?

The curtains billowed again, this time outward through the opening in the floor-to-ceiling glass. Then they hung still. Still as the flowers in the blue vase.

The apartment door opened and Hughie and Grandad came in.

"What time, Grandad? What time is the surprise?" Hughie was asking.

"At four-thirty, Hughie. About half an hour from now," Xandra heard her grandfather answer.

"What surprise?" she asked her grandmother.

"You'll know at four-thirty. And you'll love it."

That was a relief. Whatever it was, she could use something cheering right now.

Gran had made tea and had unabashedly brought in more of the burnt cookies when Mom walked in.

"Ellen!" Gran said.

"Mom? What's going on?" Mom home at four o'clock on a work day? Gran surprised to see her? Xandra's glance darted from one to the other.

"This is a family occasion," Mom said, looking un- comfortable to be part of it, then smiling, determined to make it quality time, regardless. "Any tea left, Fiona?"

"Of course, Ellen. And cookies." They all laughed.

"But why are you home, Mom?"

"Your father's *Storytellers* company was videotaped in

performance at one of the schools. It's on at four-thirty."

"Mom! Dad's on TV?" Xandra felt the rush of tears to her eyes. Happy tears. "Oh Mom. That's wonderful!"

Hughie burst out of his unusual silence. "Will he get paid?" That kid had big ears as well as a big mouth, Xandra decided.

But Grandad could cope with him. "Hughie, every time your father looks into the happy faces in his school audience, he gets paid. In pure gold."

"Like a leppercorn's gold?"

"Exactly like a leprechaun's gold. You find it at the end of the rainbow."

"Are you all right, Xandra?" her mother asked.

"I'm fine." In fact, come to think of it, it was days since she had felt finer. Maybe, just maybe, the ghost would be gone forever. And she was going to see Dad performing on the stage! She jumped up to turn on the TV.

"Not for ten minutes yet, dear," her mother protested. Then she laughed and hugged her excited daughter.

It was the longest ten minutes in Xandra's life.

"Give it all you've got, Dad," she breathed, as the show began.

The children's theatre company's logo came on — Canada Geese were flying across the screen, against the noisy and enthusiastic background of hundreds of kids released from lessons to have fun with *The Storytellers*.

And then . . . a loved voice was singing that swinging, swaying waltz melody that had been haunting his daughter:

"DON'T touch my BERRies
And DON'T touch my TREES . . . "

"That's it! That's the song he wouldn't finish," she sang out, flinging her arms wide as she leapt up to waltz around the room.

And there was the storyteller — Dad — in tights and belted tunic, fingering a mandolin while he led the singing.

Then the TV screen filled with the title. In decorative print like a child's storybook.

MUDDLEHEAD MIDAS
and the
MYSTICAL SPRING
by
Connal Warwick & Jeremy Jones

"He wrote it." Her voice was a thrilled whisper.

"Jeremy writes the music for Connal's lyrics," Grandad informed them. HE knew all about it.

"But why — " Why hadn't they told HER? About her own father! That her actor dad had written a musical fantasy, songs and all.

It was her mother who answered, "Your dad wanted it to be a surprise . . . " The lively burst of the opening number saved her from further explanation. But why had Gran been surprised to see Mom? Because Mom hadn't planned to see it. And Xandra knew why.

This was keeping "your head in the clouds" when it should be crunching numbers so your children could go to college and not have their heads in the clouds. But she *had* come. Xandra thought about her dad's smile when he had sung the lines to her. He *had* wanted it to be a surprise.

"SSHHHHH!" she warned Hughie before giving in to the magic of the stage.

Against a painted forest backdrop, the story opened on the Mystical Spring, a pool at the foot of a tree where a wood nymph danced in green garments as wispy as the moss that hangs from trees in the rainforest. But she was caught in a spell that made her unable to speak her own thoughts — she could only echo the words of the others. It was Echo's old spell, the myth Xandra had always loved, and maybe identified with. But this was a new wood nymph, Eco Green — and the young man Xandra glimpsed hiding in the woods, watching, adoring Eco Green, was a forester's son, with a backpack and birding glasses.

As her dad's magic unfolded, she could see that the fearsome, bellowing king, Muddlehead Midas, was a new Midas. He was caught in the old spell, too. Everything he touched turned to gold. But he was threatening to turn into gold the things of Xandra's own world — the precious things of the natural world in the Northwest. Oh, no! He was threatening to turn birds' eggs, and deer and berries, and even the trees and the magical pool into gold. Then, the song came from the forest, warning the king — the song that had haunted her since her dad had sung a snatch of it. *"DON'T touch my BERRies and DON'T touch my TREES . . . "*

Now, the forester's son was rousing the Ravens, the raucous black birds who snatched up anything that glittered, to stage an attack on the gold-glittering Midas and terrify him into getting rid of his golden touch. But he, a human, couldn't talk to the Ravens. Eco Green must help. She must talk to the Ravens.

But she couldn't speak her own thoughts. Xandra's hand flew to her throat. She was Eco Green, struggling to find her voice. "You must, you must!" Xandra willed her. Eco Green, driven by her desperation to save her Mystical Spring and her forest world, FOUND HER VOICE. She broke the spell. Talked to the Ravens. Who terrified the Midas so totally that he washed off his Golden Touch. The forest would stay green forever. Xandra slumped, limp, as the chorus sang out "*DON'T touch my BERRies and DON'T touch my TREES*..." Tears of joy were running down Xandra's cheeks.

"That was wonderful. I'm going to phone Dad," she informed her mother.

"He'll be on the road now. Let's send a telegram . . . from the whole family," her mother answered. Did Xandra actually hear a hint of admiration for her dad in her mother's voice?

"I'll attend to it, Ellen." Grandad got briskly to his feet. "I have to go anyway." Then he added. "It has occurred to me that artists may be more valuable to society than even scholars and business people." He held his hand up like a traffic policeman's. "However, I am admittedly reluctant to suggest that Connal Warwick and/or Fiona Finnigan Leprechaun O'Hare, the lady of the many former lives, could possibly be even a quarter as useful as I am."

Before the laughter subsided, it was Mom who was holding up her hand. "Ron and Fiona, I don't think you have any idea how valuable you both are to this family — your son's family." Then she fled to her room as she burst into tears. Poor Mom!

"Connal's wonderfully gifted," Gran said, dabbing at her eyes with a purple scarf.

"And he'll get paid!" shouted Hughie. With the last, loudest word.

TWELVE

It woke her up in the middle of the night — the idea that her father had had her in mind when he had written Eco Green, the girl who was unable to express her *own* thoughts. It was just a feeling she had, a vague feeling; but Dad had always sensed how things were with his daughter, hadn't he? Maybe he knew that Xandra couldn't express *her* own thoughts — that she always said what she thought other people wanted to hear. And that she had a desperate need to find her own voice.

"Dad, I'll do it," she breathed, there in her dark room. "I'll make myself say what I have to say to Hilary. And if she doesn't want me for a friend — THEN I'll worry about that.

But by late morning, when she was on her way to Sea Village, risking her one and only hope of a friend seemed a little desperate. Maybe even a bit theatrical?

Not that Grandad seemed to notice. It was he, and not Gran who was taking her to Granville Island. As they walked along the seawall, he turned to her and said, "Well, young lady, how would you like to go off on a week's cruise?"

"Cruise?" Instant alarm was lessened by the thought that a sailor like Grandad would never send her off on a cruise in *The Tortoise* with Hilary in charge of things. Of course, he, like Hilary, would think that if you had been scared at sea, then you ought to get right back out there on the sea again. But he would see to it that you were safe. Xandra was so sure of it that she dared to start feeling excited. A cruise? Had he been talking to Mr. Olsen? "Grandad! A cruise?"

"On the *Kanu*. She's a splendid yacht."

He sounded so excited that she blurted out a wild hope. "Are you going too?"

"I am. Your friend's father invited me. So you had better prepare yourself for ship's discipline. No going out in a dinghy when a small craft warning has been posted."

Ship's discipline was fine with Xandra, who had no burning desire to go out again in a dinghy at all. "That's super." With ship's discipline, Hilary would not be so free to "handle" her father's ulcer.

But, would Hilary want to have her along on a cruise once she had heard that Xandra believed in ghosts? She glanced up at her grandad.

His eyes were shining. "I haven't been out on a real cruise in years," he told her.

Maybe . . . maybe she shouldn't tell Hilary about the ghost. Grandad was so happy at the prospect of a cruise that it would be terrible if Hilary thought she was crazy and wouldn't want the Warwicks along. How could she do that to Grandad? On the other hand, if she didn't say what she had to say to Hilary, she'd have lost the lesson that Dad believed was important enough to write a play about.

Yet, if she did say it and the cruise was called off, Grandad was going to be devastated, and Hilary would hate her forever. Why did life get so complicated?

Then they were on the ferry, with Xandra hanging on white-knuckled while the other passengers were as carefree as gambolling dolphins. There was the market, with people thronging the wharf areas — people and pigeons and sea gulls; while below them reflections trembled in a shining, shape-shifting mirror world. Xandra trembled with them.

She was thankful to see that H.H. merely waved from up there on the wharf when she gave him a "not now" sign. He'd turn up when the time came. That was one thing you could count on in this world — H.H. turning up.

Hilary was waiting for them on the wharf above the houseboats. "Hi," she greeted them with a wave.

"Good morning, Hilary," Grandad said as she ran up.

"I can see you already know about the cruise," she said to Xandra, her eyes as bright as Grandad's. "But you don't know about another surprise I have for you."

Surprise? Being surprised had not exactly been fun and games lately on Granville Island.

Then she was on the houseboat, out on the sun deck with the blaze of nasturtiums and geraniums and fuchsias and boats breezing by, and the two men poring excitedly over a big chart in the living room.

And Hilary was walking out onto the sun deck. *With Xandra's shoulder bag.*

"Hilary! Where did you get that?"

"The Coast Guard had it. They called Dad. They knew one of us had had it when they found us, but they couldn't remember which one. They forgot to send it on the ambulance with us. So Dad picked it up, and here it is. Surprise!"

Xandra took the bag and looked inside. The pendant was there. She just felt weak.

When she looked up and saw H.H. on the wharf, she waved unobtrusively to him from the rail. *Wait.*

She could hardly think. Wait for what? What was she going to tell them? Now that she had the pendant back, something else might happen.

"Let's leave the ship's officers to plot the course," Hilary said, full of her bright ideas. "Dad? Maybe the crew could have its lunch at Isadora's?"

"Be my guests," he said, giving Hilary some money. He was as excited as Grandad was. Xandra guessed that they both loved heeling over until the sea was washing in over the slanting deck; maybe they didn't even care if you capsized. "Be back by three," he said.

"Thanks, Dad," Hilary sang out as they took off. "Oh, oh. Him," she added with a nod toward the bench where H.H. was waiting.

"Yeh." Xandra picked up her bag. "And, please, don't get mad at him. I asked him to hang around. He has something for you, from that artist. And I . . . I promised to tell him something. Tell you both something." She picked up her bag.

"Oh?" Hilary wanted an explanation now.

"Let's walk over to the benches by Isadora's." Where I'll kill myself, her anguished tone suggested. She beckoned to H.H.

"About what?" Hilary persisted. "You haven't got pneumonia or something and can't go on the cruise?"

"No. I haven't got pneumonia."

Then they were at the reeds by the stream in front of Isadora's; and Hilary, obviously impatient, was ignoring H.H. A small white dog had trotted across the little wooden bridge from the condominium area. He saw them and stopped.

Now the dog took off across the bridge. As if it had been shot at.

The neighbours' dog! Whenever Flora Lee had appeared back there in the shadows at the bottom of the garden, the neighbour's dog had taken off as if it had been shot at. Then it would sit down at the edge of that little place. And now, this dog was sitting at the other end of the wooden bridge warily watching.

Mouth open, watching the dog, Xandra caught a

scent. Pinks! Like the aromatic scent of those pinks in the rock garden where the pendant had been hidden so long ago. She made herself breathe steadily. But the back of her neck was prickling. Again, somebody was doing something weird. And she, Xandra Warwick knew who it was.

She noticed that Hilary was eyeing her. "What's going on?" She looked around apprehensively. "Not more weird stuff?" She eyed H.H.

"That's . . . what I have to tell you."

H.H. thrust the cardboard tube at Hilary. "That artist sent you this."

Hilary started twisting out the sketch. "A sketch of me in my killer whale shirt," her squeal was pure delight. "It's great!"

"Yes," Xandra agreed, thankful for the reprieve. But that's all it was. A reprieve. "She did one of H.H. too."

"Yeh," H.H. admitted. "But Xandra wants to tell us something. Right, Xandra?"

"Right." But *wants to* was not quite right. *Had to* was more like it. She had to tell Hilary the truth.

The pendant was back. Flora Lee was back. And maybe she was going to be stuck with being haunted for the rest of her life. She could see her life before her. No friends. Weird things happening to people when she was around them. But she was not going to be stuck with pretending for the rest of her life!

Then it hit her. Maybe she didn't have to be stuck with either — the ghost or pretending. Gran had told her that Mr. Lee had died. That was very sad for Mrs. Lee. But maybe it was very good for their lost, lonely, little ghost daughter. And if Xandra believed in one

ghost, she could believe in two. A big ghost looking
for that little ghost. And once her father found her,
Flora Lee wouldn't be alone any more. So she
wouldn't have to haunt Xandra.

"There's something you need to hear," she told
Hilary; though it was Flora Lee she was really talking
to. There was something Flora Lee needed to hear.
And sometimes it was more important to be a friend
than to hang on to one. "Look, Hilary, this won't take
five minutes, but maybe you should sit down."

"Okay." Hilary made an effort to look patient as
she settled down on the grass. But she looked at H.H.
as she said, "Xandra, if this is any more of that poltergeist stuff, I'd better warn you. The next time I get
pushed or clobbered or anything, I'm going to find
out who did it and they're going to get a lot worse
than a fish in the ear."

"I may not be able to do anything about that, Hilary
but I'm going to try," said Xandra. "When I was four,
we moved to a house at the edge of town. And . . . "
And as she got into her story, she found herself
caught up in the drama of Flora Lee; she could see it
all, like a dream sequence in a movie, with Flora Lee
moving through an ethereal dance routine.

It was Hilary's fidgets that brought her back to
reality, to the reason she was telling this story; they
brought her back to the sad, angry, lost little ghost
girl, who was listening to her right now.

"Flora Lee was always angry about her parents
leaving her," Xandra said. "She never knew that they
left her because they couldn't bear to go back to
where they had all been so happy. But now her father

is dead, like her. So — "

Xandra opened her mouth to go on. But it just stayed open because . . .

. . . Because — now — Flora Lee *knew* that her father was dead, like her, and that he was looking for her. And Xandra also knew that Flora Lee said, "Good-bye," though there was no sound.

Flora Lee was going off to search for her father. But not before she settled one score.

Without warning, Hilary toppled over. "Hey!" she cried out. She jumped up. "Somebody pushed me!"

And at that moment . . .

The small white dog came trotting back across the wooden bridge.

"I think . . . I think . . . the ghost is gone." Xandra scarcely breathed it. "Maybe she's gone to search for her father . . . I do think she's gone."

"Me too!" Hilary snapped; and her eyes seemed to be shooting off blue sparks. "I've had it with you and your ghost."

"I'm sorry you're mad. And I'm sorry you're leaving, Hilary," Xandra said, feeling just a bit tragic. "I'm not weird. I didn't like what happened. But it happened. And now it's over . . . I think. Anyway, you do know that it wasn't H.H. doing those things." She found she was blinking back tears.

Hilary looked at H.H. "I know it wasn't you, H.H. But there aren't any ghosts, so somebody did it! I just don't know who," she finished lamely. Then she turned on Xandra. "For heavens sake, Xandra, don't start crying," said the girl, who looked like *she* might start crying.

"You mean . . . you're not going?"

"I mean I'm not dumb. Strange things do happen,
sometimes." Her good spirit was resurfacing. "Xandra,
you're like your gran. You can easily believe in . . . in
strange stuff. And you'll probably end up getting hypnotized and finding out you were a witch in one of
your past lives. Better a witch than a beaver."

"And you're like my grandad," Xandra retorted,
even as she sagged with relief at the way things were
turning out. "If Gran tries to get him to believe what
she believes, he just pats her hand and says, 'You sail
your boat and I'll sail mine.' And they have a great
time together anyway."

"I like that. You sail your boat and I'll sail mine.
So you go ahead and believe in ghosts, Xandra, but
don't try to get me to believe in them. So . . . what are
you going to do with that pendant?" she asked. "I dare
you to get another chain and wear that ghostly thing."

"Well, dare away. But I'm not going to wear it. I'm
giving it to Gran. She likes this kind of stuff. I don't."

"She won't wear it," Hilary protested. "There's
not enough purple in it."

"No. But," Xandra turned happily dramatic, "there's
energy in it . . . power from The Other World . . . "

"All that energy and power is making me hungry.
Come on, Xandra . . . H.H. . . . let's go to Isadora's
and get some food."

When H.H. smiled, he didn't look geeky at all,
Xandra thought.

She was smiling, too. She and Hilary were going to
be friends. They were going on a cruise. And they'd do
lots of other things together, too. You could do anything,
say anything, cope with anything if you had a friend.

But you couldn't have a friend — not a real friend, if you didn't hold on to your own dream and find your own voice, to speak up and say what you felt.

"And," Hilary went on, "we have to be back home by three so we can get in on some of the planning."

It was going to be a fantastic summer.